I0620926

Slack

Rook & Ronin Book Four

HaUSS

Dedication

You misunderstood men, you…
We love ya!

JA HUSS

CHAPTER ONE

I cross Park Avenue at a full run and head down Stout where it intersects with Broadway. My breathing is not even heavy. It's difficult to get a decent run in this flat city without the Coors Field steps to challenge me. My building looms in front of me, contributing to the Denver skyline. This pre-dawn run is the only peace I'll get today, might as well enjoy it. I pick up my pace and run harder, desperately trying for the endorphin rush, but there's just not enough distance. Not enough incline. Not enough time.

I slow as I cross the street and then walk up to the doorman. He welcomes me back with small talk and gratitude for the Christmas tip I authorized via my personal accountant. I ignore his *thank yous* and get in the elevator, then key in the code to the penthouse so the doors will close.

I count the floors as they ding. Too many. But it lets me feel removed from society so I don't hold it against the condo. The doors open right into my space, but it's not the actual condo. It's a hallway that has a pet mat—which at this moment has a kneeling and naked pet on top of it—a closet, and a poinsettia plant that someone who is not me, put there.

Most likely it was my mother and most likely it her subtle way of reminding me that midnight mass is tonight.

I have no idea why she bothers. I never go. I haven't gone to church since I graduated high school. As a Jesuit student I was required to attend mass and take theology but that was the very first change I made in my adult life. No more church. I'm not a believer. It's been almost eight years, so the fact that my mother continues to ask me to attend midnight mass with her every Christmas Eve I'm in town, is just annoying.

I shake it off because she does her best, I guess. I'm weird. Her only child is probably a huge disappointment. She probably figures she'll never get a wedding out of me. She'll never have grandkids.

It's gotta sting.

"Stay here, pet. I'll be back later."

The girl on the pet mat says nothing, which is mandatory. I do not want to hear them speak. At all. Not one word. Some moaning, some squealing, small whimpering and tears during punishments—all that is fine. But if they talk, they are asked to leave and they never come back.

If I were to describe my condo with one word it would be sterile. The furniture is white with black accents, the walls are a light gray that looks a little too pink for my tastes, and the view is visible from the front door as you walk in.

The penthouse terrace faces west so I have an unobstructed view of the mountains. I close the door and walk quickly to the shower, wash off, and then pull on a pair of jeans and make my way back to the kitchen. I press the button on the machine and it spits the one-cup instabrew out into a mug. I take it and a bowl of cut strawberries over to the dining table and swipe my finger across the tablet so I can read the Wall Street Journal after

I finish with the pet.

I walk back over to the door, open it, and then bend down and whisper in the pet's ear. "Count to ten, come in, shut the door behind you, and then crawl to the table." I walk back over to the table and take my seat. Her ten seconds are up and she stands, walks through the door, closes it softly behind her then drops to her knees and crawls across the hard stone tiles.

She never once looks at me.

Another rule.

Her hair is long and blonde. It hangs down and brushes against the floor as she crawls. When she reaches me, I open my legs and pat my thigh. She rests her cheek on my leg and assumes the position.

The position is kneeling, legs open, head straight, hands on her thighs. My pat is a command she knows, so that's why she rests her head on my leg. She's been here about two dozen times. I have no idea what her name is, how old she is—other than legal age—where she lives, what she does, what this means to her, or why she does it.

And I could care less about any of that personal stuff. My assistant in LA sets all this up for me and I typically have no contact with the pets beyond fucking them, and occasionally I take one out to eat or to a function that requires a date. Not often though. I prefer to do almost everything alone.

"Are you hungry?"

She nods.

I pick up a small piece of cut strawberry from the bowl in the center of the table. "Open."

She lifts her head slightly and opens her mouth. I place the wet fruit on her tongue and she closes her mouth and chews slowly, then licks her lips to get a drop of juice.

I like that. I'm hard already. This girl is a fair submissive. She made a few minor mistakes when she first came, but over the past few months she's learned fast. She takes the punishments, she likes it in the ass, and she comes for me on command.

She's good.

Good enough, anyway.

She's about as far away from my type there is. Because my type is Rook. Dark hair, dark eyes—I make allowances for Rook's blue eyes because they are striking. Much too beautiful to dismiss as a fault.

But the pets are never dark. The pets are always light. Blonde or red. It's a requirement.

"More?" I ask.

She nods again and I detect a small smile forming on her lips as I pluck another strawberry piece from the bowl and place it on her tongue. She moans this time and I wonder how real that is. Does she enjoy this?

"Stand up." I command. She obeys immediately and I slip my fingers between her legs. She's very wet. "Good girl," I tell her in a low voice. Her skin prickles, like I just gave her the chills. I open my palm and flatten it against her sex, then push two fingers inside her. This makes her moan again. "Kneel, please." She does, and my fingertips slip out of her pussy and drag her wetness up her stomach and across her breasts as she moves. She's got her head down again. I tip her chin up with my finger that is still slick with her juices and then press it against her lips. She opens and licks, then wraps her lips around my finger and gently sucks—her tongue caressing it seductively. I slouch back in the hard dining room chair and unbutton my jeans. "Proceed."

She leans in and grabs the zipper with her teeth,

6

chancing a quick look up to see if I'm pleased.

I give her nothing, so she looks back down at her task. Once the zipper is down she leans back and waits. The first time she did this, she made the mistake of touching me. Her palms flattened against my thighs and she got a swift smack on the ass with the riding crop, hard enough to make her yelp.

"You're a good pet."

She sighs with satisfaction as I grab my dick and free it from the jeans. "Begin," I whisper.

She's eager and a moment later her hot breath is teasing me as her face moves slowly towards her goal. Her lips part and then her tongue darts out and licks my tip. Her whole mouth opens up and she descends on me, the combination of her warmth, wetness, and desire makes my balls tighten and my shaft stretch. My left hand clamps down on her head while my right hand slides down across her throat. She hesitates slightly. I've never touched her throat before and I've got her wondering, no doubt. Breath play is not something I do and if she read her contract carefully, she'd know that. But she remains stiff until I remove that hand. I force her down on my cock, a punishment for disappointing me, and then try that throat again. She stiffens and then gags because she's lost her concentration. I ease up on her head and let her pull back, but she dives back in before I have a chance to dismiss her.

This one catches on quick.

I've dismissed her before. The first two times she came over. Once for gagging and once for talking. Since then she's held the gag reflex in check and she never again uttered a word.

Like I said, quick learner.

7

"I don't like the gagging, pet." She opens her mouth further and devourers my cock, burying it into her throat. I reach down and palm her neck again, feeling for the muscle strain as I force her to take more. She breathes through her nose, my hard thickness blocking her airway, and then I explode into her, the semen bursting out as I press my hand against her throat. She swallows... *once*, *twice*.

I let go of her head and she withdraws. Licking her lips and eyes cast down. "Look up," I command.

She lifts her head, but her eyes do not meet my gaze. She's not allowed to do that either. I stare at her for a few moments. Her make-up is smeared down her cheeks from the tears.

"Sit in my lap."

She stands, sniffling a little, and perches herself on my thighs. I reach around and play with her clit and this makes her forget her tears and begin to moan. "I'm going to leave you frustrated today. Would you like that?"

She nods out a yes.

"Good. If you want to come back later, I'll be here at ten."

This is not customary. I rarely make dates. Pam, my assistant does almost all the scheduling. The pet turns her head to the side, almost like she's about to ask me something. But then she faces forward again and keeps her mouth shut.

"You were a good pet today. If you come back tonight I'll show you how much I appreciate your obedience." I push her up and smack her behind. "Go."

Her ass sways slightly as she walks. Not in a flaunting way—she knows better than to tease me. I spanked her for that the last time she was here. No, this is just her natural sexy gate. She is sexy, I conclude. Even though her cheeks are not red with my hand prints, I like the view from behind.

"Ten," I remind her. "Unless you have plans for tonight?"

She stops at the door, probably stunned that I asked her a question. She shakes her head no, and then she takes a deep breath. Uncertain. Wondering if I took that as a *no, I'm not coming.* Or *no, I have no plans.*

"You have plans?" I ask to clarify.

She shakes her head no.

"I'm surprised, really. You're pretty."

Why does she do this? Why does she participate in this… this… this *totally* fucked up arrangement? And it's not the submissive thing that makes me wonder. Lots of women enjoy being submissive. That's not weird. What's weird is that she allows me to treat her like she's worthless. I've never understood this. I love it, don't get me wrong. I love that there are women who will put aside their own needs and submit to my whims. Not speak to me, not touch me with their hands—and still pleasure me sexually. But what could she possibly get out of it? More often than not I pay no attention to them. I've left this pet sitting on the mat outside the door for hours. Twice. And once I never even showed up. I have no idea how long she stayed waiting because I couldn't even be bothered to check the security footage to find out.

I am the first to admit that my rules are unreasonable. My behavior is atrocious. My indifference is derogatory. But if the pets don't care, why should I?

She contemplates my statement, probably wondering if she's supposed to actually address it. But she decides correctly that I really do not give fuck and she exits quietly.

I tuck my dick back into my pants and reach for my coffee and take a sip.

What a productive morning.

I grin widely.

The coffee's still hot, I ran, I got a blowjob, and I'm ready for whatever the fuck this stupid Christmas Eve decides to throw at me.

Life could be worse.

CHAPTER TWO

My phone rings and I glance over at the screen. "Fuck." I pick it up and swipe my fingers. "What's up?"

"I need a small, you available?"

He sounds paranoid and this means I can mess with his head, so I take a loud slurping sip of coffee and swallow. "I have a date tonight. Will we be finished by ten?"

"Shut the fuck up and come get me, you freak. I'm at DIA, west terminal, parking garage level two, behind a blue station wagon, near the south elevators. Do the call and I'll come out when you get here."

"Merc, I swear, if you complicate my life today, I'll be—" I get the three quick beeps on my phone that tells me the line went dead. I hope he hung up on me and didn't get caught in whatever scheme he's involved in.

Goddammit. I walk to the bedroom and pull on a white t-shirt. I wanted to wear a suit today but Merc will be looking like a vagrant, and a suit would make us stand out. So this it is. I open the patio door and check the temperature, it's still mild. Not as warm as it was when I was running this morning, the cold front is getting closer. But still forties, easy.

I grab my leather jacket and stuff my keys and phone

11

into the pockets. There's a small bag sitting on the pet mat and I bend down and pick it up. What the hell? She's leavening me things? I open it up and I'm accosted with the scent of homemade cookies. I take one out and bite, chewing as I wait for the elevator. They're pretty good. When the ding comes and the doors open I toss the bag back down on the pet mat and leave it for later.

Someone gets on a few floors below. Woman with a dog. She nods and I'm just about to turn my head and ignore her when Rook comes to mind. I smile and dog lady starts chatting about the weather. "Yes," I say, agreeing with her about the coming snow. See, this is why I ignore people. They talk to you if you acknowledge them. But Rook is friendly, so maybe she likes friendly guys? Ronin is friendly. And Spencer even more so. So I figure if I want Rook to like me, then I should try to emulate the other people in her life whom she likes. Ronin is her number one and Spencer is not far behind. She's always smiling with Spencer. He makes her laugh. Ronin makes her blush.

And me? I make her uncomfortable.

The elevator doors open and I nod at the chatty dog woman as she gets off. "Nice talking to you," I say amicably. She sets her dog down and hurries off, calling out a good day to me as she goes.

Well, that wasn't so bad.

The doors close and I descend to the parking garage and then make my way over to the Bronco, Rook still on my mind. I sigh as I picture her with Ronin. Why? Why him? Of all people? I like Ronin these days, he's not a bad guy. But why does he always get the fucking girl?

I met Ronin on his first day of high school. Spencer and I grew up together—he lived across the street from us in fact. We both went to St. Margaret's, so his first day of high school was something I looked forward to. Since I had my truck, I picked him up on his first day of ninth grade. Ronin came along as part of the package. I'm two years older than them, so I was in high school when Spence and Ronin were putting the Team together back at St. Margaret's.

Spencer got in the front seat, looking like a fucking linebacker for the Broncos—that's how big he was at fifteen, and Ronin got in the back, looking like a fucking Calvin Klein underwear model.

He was too young for that kind of modeling back then, but I know for a fact he did jeans and sportswear. His life was bizarre. And not in a bad way, but bizarre in a way that makes people jealous. He never spent the entire school year in actual school. And our high school was pretty strict about attendance, but did Ronin Flynn have to abide by the rules? No. Antoine fucking Chaput stepped in and glossed it all over so Ronin could leave every month or so for a few days to go shoot in New York or LA for his own work, or just travel with Antoine and Elise for Chaput Photography. The girls went wild over him. Our school was co-ed, but the boys and girls were separated for classes and the only time we got to mix was during lunch or at afterhours events.

Sitting with Ronin at lunch was enough to give any guy an inferiority complex, but add my social limitations to that mess and it was torture for me.

I get in the Bronco and start her up. It's not too cold so I don't bother letting the engine warm up, just put her in gear and head out towards Denver International. The drive is long. They made this airport a while back and it was in the middle of the Denver expansion. That was their excuse for why the fucking place had to be an hour outside of the damn city. It takes forever to get there. Literally in the middle of nowhere. Which means I have all this time to sit and stew on why Ronin gets the girls and I get the pets.

Fucking pets.

Not that I don't enjoy them, I do. I like the sex, they're good at it. And the girl this morning is not bad. She's pretty in her blonde way. She's trying hard to please me. She keeps her mouth shut. She's acceptable.

But I want Rook.

Rook is all those things the pet is, times a million. She's obedient, she's submissive, she's beautiful—far, far more beautiful than the girl this morning. And Rook is smart. She might not think so, she's always down on herself about school. But she's smart in all the ways that count. Plus, she likes to run. I love that. Love that. I miss her running with me so fucking bad. It kills me to run alone after having her as a partner for half the year. I hate it. It takes all the joy out of it.

I miss her.

I really, really miss her.

The traffic on I-70 is horrific—must be an accident up ahead. Colorado has the worst drivers. They say California drivers are bad, but that's not true. California drivers know what they're doing. They might speed the hell down the freeway, but they can cut over six lanes of traffic, find a song on the iPod, check their teeth in the mirror, and flip off the slow driver they're passing without even blinking.

Here—every day is a major fuck-up on the freeway. And there is really only one way to get to DIA from Denver unless I want to drive up north and cut back around on the toll road. And I don't. So I sit in traffic.

Back to Ronin. God that guy just pissed me off from the minute I met him. Getting into my truck, chatting and laughing with Spencer like they're best friends since birth or something.

I was Spencer's friend all growing up. Spence comes from money, like me. My parents inherited our house and Spencer came from the same situation. Our families have lived across the street from each other for close to fifty years. But there was Ronin, inserting himself between us like be belonged, even though he wasn't even from Park Hill. He was from fucking Five Points. The slum of Denver. And he was practically the son of a porn photographer.

I mean, looking at it objectively, that's exactly what the situation was.

I inch past the accident and finally the freeway opens up just past the 225. I get over in the right lane so I can get on Pena. One long ass road that only goes one lonely ass place. The airport.

But every girl at school loved Ronin the minute he got out of the truck that day. It was like something out of a movie where the action is all slow-mo, the dude drags his hand through his perfectly messed up, yet still coiffed, hair, and all the girls drop their Trapper-Keepers and gawk at him with their mouths open.

I hated him.

I still might hate him a little. Maybe even more than a little.

He's just lucky that loyalty is my number one moral value. Maybe my only moral value. I do, after all, steal, cheat, lie, and lust. I have most of the vices covered. But for some reason, my whole worldview begins and ends with this absolute dedication to Spencer and Ronin. I'm not even sure how it started since I hated him immediately.

But it's there. I can't not be loyal to Ronin. I simply can't change it. We're bound together in this life whether we want to be or not. I'm sure he hates me as well. Maybe even more, since he knows Rook loves me in her own way and there's nothing he can do about it.

DIA eventually shows up off in the distance. They say the white peaked roof is supposed to remind people of the snow-capped Rocky Mountains, but it looks like a some futuristic circus tent of you ask me. I always get a strange craving for cotton candy when I come here.

I get in the lane for the west terminal garage and then follow the road around to the ticket station. Fucking Merc. Making me get a ticket and pay for parking. Why can't he just show up like normal people instead of being all paranoid and stealthy? Now security will have my plates when I leave because I have to stop at the exit and pay as they take pictures of my car. If he would just stand out at *Arrivals* like everyone else, then I could swoop in, pick his ass up, and swoop back out. No plates. No pictures. No payment.

I pull up in front of the stop gate and roll my window down so I can take a parking ticket. The gate lifts and I drive through, trying to get my bearings on which way is north so I can find the south elevators on level two.

In California, west equals the ocean. In Denver, west equals the mountains. I find the mountains so I know where south is, and then take the ramp up to level two. This place is packed since it's Christmas Eve and there are holiday travelers everywhere. Kids are crying, moms and dads are stressed, and grandparents are happy to be with them, even though it's an all-out nightmare trying to get in and out of this garage.

I drive past the south elevators, looking for a station wagon and come up short. So I try the old-fashioned method. I roll the window down and yell, "Merc!"

Every set of stressed-out eyeballs turns at my call and stares at me.

I stare back and have to tuck down the urge to say something nasty.

Then the passenger door opens and a man slides in, half ducking down thinking no one can see him, and tugging on his hat to cover his eyes. Merc is a huge guy, at least six foot four and two hundred pounds. So him thinking he can duck in the seat and hide himself is almost funny. His hazel eyes are darting all over the place, checking the parking lot. His hand rubs the stubble on his chin, and his cropped brown hair is covered by a trucker hat that proclaims he's a bacon lover.

"Good going, Rutherford. Just call out my fucking name in one of the busiest airports on the planet on one of the busiest days of the year."

"You said call you."

"No, I said, do *The Call* Ford. Not just scream out my name."

"I do not scream. And the last call we had together was a duck. Quacking out a duck call in an airport parking garage is gonna be less conspicuous than your name?"

"Whatever," he says as he turns to check behind us like the paranoid freak he is, "just drive."

"Well now we have to stop at security to get our fucking pictures taken, so this is all moot anyway. You should've stayed in *Arrivals*."

"Fuck that, I saw a few suspicious people back there. One on the plane and one in baggage. I went to baggage because it's what people do and I was blending in, plus I wanted to see if this guy would follow me. And he did."

"Let me guess, he picked up bags from baggage as well? Suspicious."

He sneers his lip at me in typical Merc fashion. "Don't patronize me, just take me to your rig. I got a smallish-big, I said."

"You said you have a small, Merc. Not some smallish-big."

"Yeah, well, think of it as a biggish-small then. Roll with it, dude."

I'm gonna regret this, I can already tell. "Nice to see you again, Merc."

He grunts. People think I'm anti-social? This guy, he's the anti-social one. He's OK one on one, but get this asshole in a group and I won't take responsibility.

I make my way down to the first level and follow the signs to the exit. Since it's a busy day, I wait in line for ten minutes as every car is photographed and matched to the picture they took at the parking garage stop gate. They do that under the guise of collecting the fee money to use the garage, But really, they are just cataloging your vehicle in case you're a terrorist.

"My rig's up in Fort Collins still. I have a place there."

"Perfect," Merc says as he lights a cigarette. He blows the smoke out of his nose and mouth at the same time. "I got a gun deal up in Cheyenne later, so that's perfect. You can take me up to Wyoming, right? I mean, you have no plans today. It's Christmas Eve for Christ's sake."

I shoot him a look for the blasphemous humor. "I said I have a date at ten."

"Yeah, but that was a joke right?" I look over at him and he's got one of those *you-fuck-with-me-I'll-fuck-with-you-*

back grins on his face.

I glare at him.

"You owe me, Ford. So just get over it. You're in."

"Fine, but this is beyond my debt, so you owe me a *big* once this is over. What's the job, anyway?"

"Some senator's sixteen-year-old daughter was kidnapped last night. Some kind of pathetic wanna-be militia in the hills between Laramie and Cheyenne is responsible. I'm going in."

He says all this like he just said I'll have eggs for breakfast. "Why not the Feds?"

"Hush, hush, you know. The girl's caught up in something bad. Drugs, sex, something. Who the fuck knows, who the fuck cares. They didn't really kidnap her from the way I see it. I figure she went on her own volition, but the senator is having none of that. All I know is that if I can get her out alive with no media involvement, I get five hundred tax-free grand." He takes a long draw on his cigarette and lets it out through his grinning teeth. "Fuckin-a, I'm in."

"What if the media gets involved?"

"Penalty," he says though a puff of smoke. "They knock off twenty percent for media fuck-ups. I'll shoot you ten grand for the lift though."

"Fuckin-a then, I'm in too." Why the hell not? Wyoming is not that far, it's Christmas Eve, I'm a total Scrooge, and my pet date is twelve hours from now. I got plenty of time to make ten grand and get back home in time to plan some Christmas Eve dirty sex.

CHAPTER THREE

It's a lot easier to get the hell out of DIA if you're going north than it is if you're going south. There's an expensive toll road almost no one uses that shuttles you past all the worst I-25 traffic and spits you out just before you hit Longmont. From there, it's a fifteen minute ride to my apartment on the southern outskirts of Fort Collins. I pull into the complex driveway and Merc starts laughing. "You live here? In this suburban singles complex?"

"Guess what I do here, Merc?"

He lights up another smoke. Fucker's been chain smoking since we left. If this was a high level job, he'd never smoke. Leaves a scent on his clothes that can give his ass away when he's sniping. So he must feel this one is no big deal.

"Eat, sleep, shit, and fuck?"

"No, I said guess what *I* do here. Not what most people do here."

He tilts his head, interested. "Fuckin tell me then."

I say nothing. Just park the Bronco in the spot numbered E33, then get out and head towards the stairs that will take me up to my third floor apartment. Merc follows behind, his cigarette still smoldering. I open the door and wave him in, then reach out and snatch the smoke from his lips and toss it over the balcony. "No smoking in my gear room."

He hands me a sly smile and I follow him in and close the door. From the entry it's just your basic shit apartment, albeit, in a luxury suburban setting. Nondescript brown couch, two dark wood end tables with matching lamps on either side. Dark wood coffee table, an over-sized chair and matching ottoman, and a dining table.

"No TV, Ford?"

"Fuck TV."

It's got three bedrooms, but only one has a bed. I open the last door on the right and let Merc walk in ahead of me. "The rig room, eh?" He says as he looks over his shoulder at me.

"You bet. The rig room."

The rig room is one long stainless steel table with one laptop and a metal stool.

"Sparse, dude."

"It's all I need."

"Right, then." He sighs his frustration with me. We've been friends since senior year of high school. He knows me well. All my strengths and all my weaknesses. "Get to it. I need info on…" he rattles off names as I pop off an electrical wall cover plate, fish around inside the wall for the end of the cable, then pull it through the hole and plug it into my laptop. I sit down in the chair and open the rig and start typing. The external drive inside the wall contains all my scripts, but its password protected and has an automatic trip. If you get the password wrong, just once, it nukes the drive.

We spend almost an hour in the rig room getting the deets on who may or may not be inside the 'compound' in the desolate hills between Cheyenne and Laramie where this girl has apparently run away to. Just as we're walking out, Merc asks the question I'm sure has been on his mind since he got here. "So what's behind door number three?"

He gives me a knowing grin.

"Books," I deadpan. *And guns.* I say to myself. Spencer has a stash here. For some reason, that paranoid fucker insists on having weapons in every place I inhabit.

"Yeah?" Merc says with interest. "Like I actually believe you have books in that fucking room, Aston. Please."

"Believe what you want." We descend back down the stairs and head to the Bronco. I know what he thinks is in there. Same thing that Rook thought was in there when she first questioned me about the apartment last fall. They both think I bring pets here, but that's not why I got the apartment. I got it to bring dates. Regular dates. Like normal girls.

I never even came close to bringing a normal girl home. Not even close.

We get in the truck and I head back towards the I-25 and get on going north. Merc is studying the notes he took back in the rig room, so I'm left with thoughts of my sorry attempt at a normal love life last October.

I gave it a shot. Thirty days. One solid month of trying. I went on eight dates. Hell, I had a shitload of inquiries on my Match.com account. I was even featured on the home page a few times. Under an assumed name, of course. Ford Aston is infamous in these parts. A one second Google search brings up thousands of hits and four years' worth of questionable shit.

No. These girls went in blind. Which speaks to the stupidity of online dating. You just never know who you're getting. Of course, I have credit cards under assumed names and most people don't. But every one of those women wanted to have sex with me after our date. Two of them made very convincing arguments with their provocative dress and dirty mouths as we got drunk at a local bar.

A threesome sorta defeats the purpose of the whole experiment, right? I can get two pets for a threesome and never have to exert an effort at conversation. So those two were a dead end the minute they walked into the bar together.

But the truth of the matter is, all those women were established. They were my age, they had degrees, they had jobs, they were looking for sex, sure. But they were also looking for all that other shit. Houses, and rings, and kids. And maybe they were just hiding their freak because it was a first date, but somehow I doubt it. Every one of them was respectable.

Every one of them was *boring*.

I ended four dates early, the two-for-one lasted until the bar closed, but that was all drinking and bull riding. Yes, FoCo is quite the rodeo town. There are no urban cowboys here, they're all one hundred percent real. And these two cowgirls took me to the only bar I know of that has bulls out back for the cowboys to ride. It was one of the most entertaining nights of my life.

But none of those girls were for me.

I gave up after thirty days and admitted defeat. I'm a freak looking for a freak. A freak that can relate to me. And the pets are the closest thing I've come to that in the way of women.

Besides Rook, of course. She's not a freak. Her sick ex tried to make her into one, but she's not a freak. She wants the fairytale I'd go for that if I could have Rook. I would. I'd give her the fairytale if she wanted it. I'm not against the fairytale. I'm not against marriage and all that shit. I'm just picky. I want what I want and I refuse to settle. I'd rather be alone than settle.

But, I sigh, there is only one Rook and her heart belongs to Ronin.

"So…" Merc tries for conversation as we head North. Cheyenne is only forty-five minutes away and there's no traffic on Christmas Eve. Hell, there's no traffic on any eve. Or any *day* for that matter. It might be the capitol of Wyoming, but I'm not sure Cheyenne even qualifies as an urban center. In fact, I think Fort Collins has double the population of Cheyenne in every season except summer when the college students go home. "How's life, Ford? You keeping busy?"

"I'm busy today, and today is the only day that matters."

"Your date tonight is your mom, right? Midnight mass and all that shit."

I laugh a little. "Please, do not even mention it. I've been avoiding her calls all fucking week."

"But she's your date, right?" he prods.

"How pathetic do you think I am?" I roll my eyes at him. "A pet I've used for a while. She agreed to come, so why not? Keeps me out of church and takes my mind of the holiday at the same time."

"Yeah, hear ya, dude. That's why I took this job, ya know? I fucking hate Christmas. Fucking hate it."

"I'm just the ride? Or you counting on backup? Do I need to call Pam and cancel the pet?"

"When we get up there, hang out for a few while I discuss the details, if that's alright. I'll let you know if I can use you. If you want in, of course."

"What if she didn't run away?"

25

He takes a long drag on the cigarette and blows it out the crack in the window. "That's what the weapons are for. But I think this girl ran away. One of the members is a guy she dated on and off for a while. Only makes sense."

"But on Christmas? I mean, *we* hate Christmas, but sixteen year old rich girls generally don't. They like big boxes wrapped in bows."

"Yeah, well, we'll see. Head east on 16th when we get into Cheyenne. The pick-up is in one of those antique malls."

I shoot him a look.

"What? It's perfect."

"Did the senator sanction the weapons too?" He doesn't answer right away and this is my first real clue that he's not as comfortable with this job as he's making it out. "What?" I ask. "What's the deal, Merc?"

He shakes his head a little, like he's thinking about lying or holding it in. But we've been friends too long, so the words come out anyway. "It's just strange. All of a sudden I start getting a string of high priority jobs from people with position, ya know? This senator. The last job was collecting a debt owed to a millionaire from Miami. Had to go to Columbia for that one. And the one before that was stealing some data from a small European government."

"Virtually, I hope?" I have insane hacking skills, like Merc here, but unlike him, I'm no soldier. I can shoot and I can fight. And if I do either of those two things you can be sure someone will end up dead by the time it's over. But I am not a soldier.

"Nah, real time dude. Boots on the ground."

"Hmmm…. maybe it was that mercenary ad you ran in *Soldier of Fortune*?"

He puffs out some smoke with his chuckle. "Hey, I was twelve."

"As if that makes it any less ridiculous." We both laugh. Fucking Merc. "Well, your name's on a list somewhere. And you seem pretty popular and the shit's sanctioned, so enjoy it I guess."

"Yeah, I guess."

Cheyenne comes into view after that and Merc takes out his notes and studies them again. I don't blame him for being paranoid. I do this shit as a side thing. This is his life. This is his day job. He has nothing else *but* this. So knowing that people with power have a list with your name on it is not comforting in the least. Because one of these days, the target and the gun might switch places.

I get off the freeway and had east on 16th like he said. This town looks like it got stuck in 1940 and nothing has changed. There's a rail yard on one side of the street and a shitload of old fashioned shops on the other. I park in front of one of the brick buildings and look up at the sign. *Roundhouse Antique Mall.*

"Why is this place even open, it's fucking Christmas Eve. Isn't everyone home with their families doing family shit and eating crap by the handfuls, wishing that everyone's kids would just shut the fuck up and fall into a post-sugar coma?"

"Jesus Christ, you really are a Scrooge. Last minute shopping, Ford. You'd know that if you ever bought a Christmas present in your life. Let's go."

I sigh as his door slams. But I give in and get out. I've got nine hours until my pet date, so what the fuck. I'll stick around for an illegal arms deal. Why not?

CHAPTER FOUR

I've never been in an antique mall. I know they exist, there's one on the west side of Denver on the side of the freeway and the sign is huge and gaudy. But I can say with one hundred percent certainty that entering that building has never crossed my mind. I'm not a snob about old things. I don't mind old things when they're mine. But as I walk down the many, many, *many* aisles in this huge-ass fucking building filled with *crap*—the first thing I think of is how many hands have touched these items.

The second thing I think is, why? Why would you come here to shop for Christmas presents?

I can only shake my head.

I follow Merc though an endless maze of booths filled with the oddest things—books, fabric, postcards, furniture, art, photographs, frames. The list goes on and on. But Merc stops in the way-way-back of the place and we end up at what appears to be a mini Cabala's store. If said store was contained within a fifteen by fifteen foot booth and it only had scratch-n-dent items.

I sigh and try my best to appear professional.

"Wait here," Merc says as he enters the booth. "I'll be back in a minute."

"Right." With Merc, be back in a minute can mean

anything from five minutes to half an hour. I pick up a knife in a basket on the counter and check it out. It's just a folding knife, but I have nothing better to do, so I flip it open and inspect the blade.

"That knife sucks," a girl's voice says from behind me.

I turn towards the voice. The child is sitting in a chair in the corner of the booth across the aisle, reading *Little House in the Big Woods*. She's about twelve, she's smiling so I can see a full mouth of braces, and her hair is up in long blonde pigtails. She's wearing a camo hoodie and some black tactical pants. "I wouldn't buy that one," she says.

I check the knife for a brand. None. Then check the blade. Dull. "Yeah, this is crap." I put it back in the basket.

"Wanna see the good ones?"

I turn again, but she's right up next to me now. "Good ones?"

"Yeah, the Emersons. We have a few left. They're a very popular Christmas present." She slides past me and opens a case, then removes a box and sets it on the counter.

"Are you allowed to open that?" I ask.

She never looks up at me, just shuffles through the box and then produces a small case. "This is my dad's booth." She nods over to the booth she came from. "That one over there is mine." And then she looks up at me with her pre-teen eyes and pouts. "I always get left out of the back-room deals too. So I know how you feel."

I laugh. "What makes you think there's some kind of back room deal going on?"

"You came in with a hunter," she says, nodding to the back room where Merc disappeared. "Hunters make deals. And since you're out here and not back there, you're not making the deal, that other guy is."

"What makes you think we're hunters?" I have no camo on and neither does Merc. "Do you see an orange vest on me?" I flap my jacket open and turn for her.

She smirks at my joking and points her finger to my face. "Not *that* kind of hunter," she giggles. "You know," she whispers, "the *hunters*."

I raise my eyebrows at her.

She raises hers back. "Your friend is buying guns from my *dad*, doofus. Do I look stupid? I know what you guys do." And then she takes her attention back to the glass case and removes an absolutely gorgeous Mini CQC and presents it to me on her flattened palm.

I take it from her outstretched hand and admire it, try the weight in my hand, then flip it open and inspect the blade. "Yeah, this is nice. How much?"

"*Welllll*," she says drawing out the word with a smile. "Since it's Christmas Eve, I can give you that for two seventy five."

I raise an eyebrow at her. "Two twenty-five is more like it."

She smiles. "Two fifty."

"Two forty."

"Deal." She sticks her hand out and for a moment I just stare at it. "Shake, doofus. That's how you seal the deal."

I look at her again, then her hand. "This knife is only worth two twenty-five, the rest is a tip for entertaining me."

Her hand remains outstretched. "Shake."

I shake and she flashes her braces at me. I open my wallet and grab the cash and hand it to her.

She shoves them in her pocket and takes the knife

and places it back in the case. "Gift wrap?"

"Nah, I might use it today."

She nods conspiratorially. "Oh, big job on Christmas Eve. Must be someone important."

What the fuck? Who lets their twelve year old daughter in on their secret arms dealing business?

"What did you get your girlfriend for Christmas? Maybe you need something else while you're here?"

"I don't have a girlfriend."

"Yeah," she says with a sigh. "You guys never have girlfriends. I used to think your work looked exciting, but then I figured out you had no lives. No offense," she says with a shrug.

"I have a life. I'm not a hunter, I'm just a helper. I have a girl who's a friend. She counts."

She squints her eyes in disbelief. "What'd you get her for Christmas?"

"Nothing. I don't do Christmas."

"Oh boy," her breath comes out in a half laugh. "You really need help. Did you at least get your mom and dad something?"

"My dad's dead and no, I just told you I don't do Christmas."

"Oh, sorry about your dad. I have a dad but no mom. Wouldn't it be nice to have both?"

She says this like one parent families are normal. That makes me a little sad. "I did have both, but my dad died two years ago."

Her head bobs in understanding. "My mom died when I was born. So…" she waves her arm around at the hunting supplies. Outdoor gear fills every bit of space in her dad's booth. As if to say, *this is what my childhood was like. All hunting, all the time*. "We're the same almost, you and I. Only opposites." She pauses to look up at me. "And I do Christmas, so that's different too. I got my dad a new longbow. We're gonna bow hunt next year if I do well at State."

"Do well at what?"

"Archery. I'm the Wyoming State champion in both trap and .22 rifle but I'm not a good enough archer yet." She looks wistfully at a bow on the wall. "There's always next year."

I just stare at her. She's like a twelve year old *La Femme Nikita*.

Fucking Wyoming. What do I expect? Shooting is practically the state sport.

"Wanna buy your mom something while you're here? Make her happy this Christmas?"

"I'm pretty sure my mother would not appreciate the finer points of an Emerson folding knife."

She laughs so all her braces show. "No, doofus. I have that booth over there. I have jewelry your mom might like. Wanna see it?" She doesn't wait for an answer, just grabs my new knife, pushes past me, and walks across the aisle where she sets the knife down and busies herself pulling out some jewelry. She lies it all down across the glass counter top and then looks up and smiles.

It's infectious, so I smile back as I walk over. What a cool kid. If all kids were like this girl, I might like them more.

"I'll help you pick. Is your mom earthy or fancy?"

"Definitely fancy."

"OK, then these ones are out." She removes a beaded necklace and some feather earrings. "How about this one?"

It's a string of pearls. "My mom would love it, but

she'd never wear it. They're not real."

"Oh, then she's classy, not fancy."

"Yeah, that's about right."

"Hold on," she says as she raises her pointing finger. "I have classy stuff too." She reaches into her pocket and produces a key for a tall metal cabinet, then unlocks it and brings out another box. "This is the good stuff. And I know just what you need." She shuffles through it and places an antique bracelet on the glass. "Those pin pricks of silver? Those are marcasite. It's not expensive, but it's pretty don't you think?"

"It is, very pretty," I answer back as I watch her. She's smiling down at the jewelry. "Are those emeralds?" I point to the little green gems.

"Yes," she whispers. And then she looks up at me. "They're small, but they're real. I bought this for my mom for Mother's Day once. It was symbolic, you know. I was missing her and wanted to give her a present. So I worked really hard to sell a lot of stuff that month and I got this bracelet from a lady who used to run a booth on the other side of the mall."

God, how sad.

"But I've been thinking about it lately and I'd like for it to go to a mother, even if it can't go to *my* mother. Do you think your mother would like this?" She lifts it up towards my face and then smiles one of those sweet, innocent little girl smiles at me.

Holy shit that almost cracks my black Grinch heart. "Absolutely," I say. "My mom would die to have this bracelet. How much?"

"I have it marked at seventy-five, but since—"

"Done." I grab some more cash from my wallet and lay it out on the counter. "Seventy-five is a steal."

"Want me to gift wrap it?" She looks up at me smiling. "I'll put it in a pretty jewelry bag. With ribbons and everything. And make a card too. I'll be fast." And before I can even answer yes, she's got the ribbon and scissors out. "You should look for something for your friend who is a girl." And then she stops mid-cut and looks up at me. "If she's just a friend, you don't give fancy things. Something small that *seems* insignificant, but really isn't. OK?"

Relationship advice from a twelve-year-old. My life couldn't be any more pathetic. But I do browse for something to give Rook. I walk inside the girl's booth a little farther and start to take things in. "What's your name?" I ask her as she busily ties ribbons to the jewelry bag.

"Sasha Alena Cherlin."

"Not Nikita then?" She laughs, like she got the joke, and that makes me like her even more. "I don't have a middle name, so Ford will have to do. Ford Aston. Sign my name on the card, OK? I have terrible handwriting. And sign yours too, so my mom knows it came from you as well."

"Awww… that's so sweet Ford. I'm gonna put little pink hearts on the tag too."

"Do it up right, Nikita."

"Sasha!" she squeals.

"Right—" I stop mid-sentence because I see the perfect gift for Rook. "I want that for the girl who is a friend."

She puts her stuff down and walks over to me. "Eric Cartman? For a girl? I'm not sure…"

"No, I'm sure. It's perfect." The little Eric Cartman figure has mirrored shades, a cop uniform, and he's

35

holding a nightstick. I laugh out loud as I picture Rook saying '*Respect ma authora-tay*' when she sees it. Can't cost more than five bucks, but this is the perfect gift for Rook. Something small that seems insignificant, but really isn't.

"Gift wrap?" Sasha asks.

"Yeah, but better leave your name off this one, OK?"

"For sure, Ford," she winks at me. "I'm a woman, I totally get it."

Just as Sasha is finishing up the gift wrap, Merc peeks his head out from behind the curtain that leads to the back. "Ford!" he yells over to me. "You can take off man, this job just got complicated."

I give him a little salute, but he's already disappeared.

"You really aren't a hunter, then?"

I look down at Sasha and smile at her. "I told you I wasn't."

"So now you have time for me to gift-wrap your knife." She grabs the case and takes it over to the little table that's doubling as a makeshift wrapping station.

"It's for me, Sasha. It doesn't need to be gift-wrapped."

"It's like a present to yourself, Ford. Just go with it."

Just go with it. I laugh. "You're kinda funny. Why are you working on Christmas Eve? Because my friend had a deal with your dad?"

"No," she says softly as she continues to wrap my knife case very carefully. "We always work until noon on Christmas Eve, just in case people wander in and need help. Like you." She looks over her shoulder and smiles before going back to her cutting and twisting. "Then we drive to my grandparents ranch near Sheridan."

"That's a long drive."

"Yeah, I love the drive. I just look out the window

and think about my grandparents and how fantastic it will be to see them. We'll have early calves this year for my 4H project and I get to stay up there and help." She stays silent for a few seconds. "I love the babies. Why are you working on Christmas Eve?" she asks as she turns with my packages.

"I don't do Christmas Eve. I usually just try to avoid the whole holiday."

"Well," she huffs, "you failed this year. You have a present to unwrap and two people you love will get a gift from you this year." She flashes me her braces and I smile back as she pushes my packages across the glass.

I stuff them in my coat pockets and shoot my finger at her, Spencer style. "Merry Christmas, Sasha Alena Cherlin. Hope you do well at State next year so you can tag that deer. And may your calf be the biggest one at weaning."

She covers her mouth to laugh and I turn around and walk away grinning.

"See ya around Ford Aston," Sasha calls out after me. "Tell your mom I said Merry Christmas too!"

Yeah, yeah… I feel like I should be saying *bah humbug*. But I don't. Because I still got a pet date in about eight hours.

CHAPTER FIVE

I think about Sasha and what her life might be like all the way back down into Colorado. Daughter of a gun dealer. Sharpshooter at age eleven. 4H calf raiser. Reader of *Little House* books.

That's quite a combination.

I'm the son of a psychiatrist, socially unacceptable genius, con-man hacker, film producer.

That's quite a combination too.

Why can't I find a twenty-five year old Sasha? Now she... is a *freak*. But in the best kind of way. Why can't I find a well-adjusted freak?

Signs for Fort Collins appear on the side of the road and I get off on Mulberry and head towards downtown. I might as well go empty out the few things I have up at Spencer's house in Bellvue before I go home. Nothing better to do. I still have seven hours until my pet date tonight. I turn right at College and head north, glancing over at Anna Ameci's when the smell of Italian food makes my stomach go ape-shit. And who do I see? Veronica Vaughn walking out of the restaurant hanging on the arm of a well-dressed man.

Hmmm.

I know Spencer and Ronnie have had their difficulties, but I haven't seen either of them since the

Shrike Bikes show ended a few weeks ago so I had no idea they broke up. I pull into one of the many empty parking spaces and get out to go butt into her business. Veronica is dressed like a runner but I know better. Ronnie does not run. The man leans down and kisses her on the cheek and then walks off, leaving her standing in front of the restaurant. He gets into a new Buick Lacrosse and drives away.

Being the good best friend that I am, I memorize the plate for future evaluation.

Veronica is daydreaming when I walk up and tap her on the shoulder.

She whirls around. "Holy fuck, Ford! What the hell? You scared the shit out of me!"

"It was intentional."

She rolls her eyes. "Well, what do you want?"

"That did not look like Spencer."

"Wow, you really are a genius," she snaps back at me. "That guy is the farthest thing from Spencer there is. He's polite, attentive, and interested. Need I say more?"

"So you and Spencer broke up? Because I'm pretty sure he has no idea you're seeing other men."

"I don't have time for this," she says pushing past me. "Spencer can go fuck himself. I'm done waiting on him to grow up. He's almost twenty-four years old and he still acts fourteen." She walks down the sidewalk towards Laurel, then stops at the light and pushes the walk button repeatedly.

I follow her.

"What are you doing? Go home, Ford."

"I was on my way to Spencer's actually. To clear out my shop apartment. Wanna come?"

"Spencer's in Denver with his family and since I'm

not part of his family, I'm gonna walk home and spend Christmas Eve with my *brothers*."

"I have the codes, I can get in everywhere."

She stops anxiously shuffling her feet and looks up at me. Spencer's Veronica is tall and tough, has big blonde hair, perpetual red lips, perpetual high heels, and a never ending E-cig.

But this other man's Veronica looks small and fragile, has no make-up on, her hair is straight and up in a ponytail, and she's not puffing.

Something is definitely wrong.

"Come with me. I'll let you snoop through all his stuff."

The light turns and her walk signal flashes, but Ronnie stands still. "Yeah, right. You'll probably record me and post it on YouTube so Spencer will break up with me."

I point my finger at her. "So, you admit you're still in a relationship with him!"

She shakes her head and then starts to walk across the street. I reach out and grab her before a car comes barreling around the corner. "Shit, Ronnie. Watch where you're walking. You die on my watch and I get the blame."

"Your watch?" she sneers.

I shrug. "I'm with you, I'm responsible for you. Which is why I'd like to know what's going on with that man you just kissed."

"I didn't kiss him, he kissed me. On the cheek."

"Same thing."

"Ford, what the hell do you want?"

"Come with me to Spencer's. I'll drop you off at home when we're done."

"Why? So you can pump me for information?"

I chuckle. But it's my diabolical chuckle. The one that says *Don't fuck with me or your life might take unexpected and unwelcome wrong turns.* "No, Ronnie. So you can talk me out of going to my FoCo apartment, looking up your man's license plate using my DMV crawler, then calling Spencer and giving him that man's address so he can show up on his doorstep tonight and start asking questions. Because that's pretty much where I'm at right now. I do not cover for anyone outside the Team."

"Right," she snaps back. "And since Spencer can't commit, I'm not on the team. I'm nobody, I'm—"

I cup my hand over her mouth because her last few words came out rather shrill and people are starting to stare. "Come with me or I do the crawl and make the call." She huffs air into my palm and then mumbles something incoherent. "What was that? Was that a yes?" She nods her head and I remove my hand. "Great, I'm parked down here."

I walk off and she follows, slowly, but she follows.

We get in the Bronco and slam our doors at the same time. She folds her arms against her chest and pouts.

"Buckle up. It's the law."

"Fuck you, Ford." But she does buckle up and I back out and continue up College until I get to the turn off for Bellvue. Ronnie stares out the window the entire thirty minute drive to the shop. I park in my old spot under the carport and glance over at Rook's custom Shrike Bike. Spencer made it for her last summer when she was doing his body art modeling campaign.

"He never gave *me* a bike you know."

"No?" I get out and Ronnie follows. The weather is still fairly mild, but the clouds are really rolling in, the threat of a storm is over and it's just about here. I look at the bike again as we walk past and then I code the lock on the back door and hold it open for Ronnie. "You know why, though, right?"

"Why what?"

"Why he never gave you a bike."

She stands in the kitchen, her arms still folded in defiance. "Because I'm not important. Because he never gives me anything. Because I'm just another fuck-buddy to him. Because he has no feelings for me. Take your pick, Ford."

"No, that's not why," I say back. "Because he doesn't want you to ride it, Veronica. Because he'd go crazy with worry if he had to think about you riding around on a motorcycle. Because you're his number one, he's just caught up in some shit right now and he doesn't want you involved. And believe me, I saw his face last summer when you almost got killed. He didn't even know how to process it."

"Right." She snorts. "He processed it just fine. He was on the road to Sturgis the very next day with you guys."

"Yeah, but that was business. You're not business, Ronnie. You're personal. He's totally in love with you."

She just stares at me for a few seconds and then blinks. "What?"

"Come on, I'll show you." I walk into the living room and then head into the hallway towards Spencer's office. "I don't have the real code for this door, but I hacked it last summer when I was bored." Veronica grunts behind me as I key in the codes. The door beeps and I push it open and wave her in.

She hesitates. "I've never been in here before, Ford."

"I know, that's why I'm taking you in here now." I

flip on the lights and she gasps, then walks across the forbidden threshold.

And gasps again. "What the hell is all this?" she asks, panning her arms wide.

I look up and try and imagine myself as her, seeing it for the first time. But I'm no good at that empathy shit, so it's no use. "Well, Ronin and I call it pussy whipped, but you can call it the *Veronica Vaughn Shrine*." I laugh privately at my joke as she takes in the walls. Every one is adorned with images of her as Spencer's body art model. He stopped using her last year, then gave that last job to Rook, so none of these are recent. But she was his model for several years—they even went to some international contests and Spencer has all those awards prominently displayed in a glass case behind his desk.

"I don't get it," she says, perplexed.

"What's not to get?"

"Why? Why the fuck does he treat me like *shit*?" She yells that last part and I wince. "Ford!" she says turning to me, her little hands clasping onto the front of my leather jacket. "Why. The. Hell? He lets me come around once a month, if that! He forgets to call me back, he snuffs me on our dates, he hasn't fucked me in three goddamned months, Ford!" She's shaking me now and I'm desperately trying to pry her hands off my coat before I start freaking out from her touching. "*Three months*! Do you have any idea how fucking horny I am! I'm gonna fuck that banker, Ford. The minute he asks, because my goddamned vibrator is broken and the fucking mall sold out of the fucking Hitachi model I like and won't be getting any more in until after fucking New Year's! I can't even find them online! Not even on eBay!"

She finally lets go and turns back to the wall art.

Holy shit. Veronica is *intense.*

But she's forgotten about me now and her attention is one hundred percent on the walls. There's six life sized photographs of her. All in body art paint, which means she's totally naked in every one of them. If it bothers her that I'm looking at her naked body, she doesn't let on. But honestly, it bothers me.

I do not want to start picturing them together.

It gives me the shivers.

"This one," she says pointing up at a photo, still a little bit hysterical, but calmer than she was about the lack of Hitachi vibrators at the FoCo Mall, "was in Austria. We won two prizes for it."

She's pointing to the one with her painted up as the cyborg chick that Rook loved so much last summer. That was Ronin's favorite picture of Rook once the STURGIS contract was all said and done. Spencer is trying to talk Ronin into letting Rook be his model for Comic-Con this year. But even though Ronnie doesn't see it yet, Spencer tells her no for the same reason Ronin will put his foot down this time as well.

No one wants their woman being displayed naked in front of thousands of men.

That's just the facts. And even though this is such a fucking no-brainer to us men with even the slightest bit of protoplasmic possessive gene, for some stupid reason, the girls never seem to get it.

Allow me to spell it out.

"Ronnie, Spencer is a man. He doesn't do feelings he does caveman. When he says 'No, Ronnie, you may not have one of my custom Shrike Bikes.' What he really means is, 'Are you fucking insane? I refuse to spend every Goddamn night wondering if you're dead in a fucking ditch somewhere. You may *not* have a bike and you will *never* get a bike with my name on it as long as I'm alive, so fucking help me, *God*.'"

"But he gave Rook a bike!"

"Yeah, because it made Rook happy and she's got Ronin to reign her in when she talks about riding it. And after she took off to Illinois alone on that fucking Shrike Bike, you see where it is now? Sitting under the fucking carport out here in the middle of nowhere, being ridden by no one. Rook will never *sit* on that bike again, let alone ride it. Ronin put his foot down and it's over. Now, do you need me to spell out why he refuses to let you model for him anymore? Because I will. I think you're smart enough to figure that shit out on your own, but I'll hold your hand tonight and not make fun of your idiocy because it's Christmas."

"Nice bedside manner, Ford. You really have a way with words." She stays silent for a few seconds, mulling this over as she looks up at her glory days as a body art model for Shrike fucking Bikes. "I'm not ready for that to be over yet. I'm just not. I'm young, I'm pretty, I'm funny and I might have a little bit of freak in me with the blood phobia, but I'm not that far away from normal. I still want to have fun and I want to have fun with *him*. I'm not ready to just give that up yet."

"No? I thought you wanted him to be serious. You can't have it both ways, Ronnie. You can't be the slutty model at the shows who attracts the buyers and lookers. You can't be the reckless biker chick with no responsibilities. You can't be the wild tattoo artist with red lips and black stilettos who will hygienically tattoo a penis if a customer walks through the door asking for it."

"I've tattooed hundreds of people and only one of

them wanted his penis adorned."

I sigh. She's so thick. "My point *is*… you can't be these things and be the kind of girl Spencer wants to settle with. Because eventually, he will settle down and when he does, he wants a wife." I shrug. I know how it sounds, but fuck it. She needs to hear the truth. "He wants dinner and kids and all that shit."

"He never said any of that to me Ford," she replies shaking her head. "He's never talked about a family at all."

"Yeah, but we were raised up together, Ronnie. I know him. We all want the same thing, we just want it in different ways. Ronin wanted to settle down right away because his life has been one exciting event after another. Spencer wants to check life out a bit, explore his options, and then settle down."

"Fuck that," she says as she stomps out of the office. I follow, flicking off the lights and pulling the door closed behind me. "If he can explore his options, then I can explore mine, too. Go ahead and tell him whatever you want, Ford. I don't care. He's hurting me with these other girls he dates. Hell, *dates*? He's fucking them and don't try and tell me he's not! So I'm done with him. I'm gonna call him tonight and tell him it's over and then tomorrow I'm meeting that guy and having a late dinner with him. And you know what, Ford? He'll probably bring me a present. Flowers or something. Spencer never buys me anything. Nothing! He might as well be you, Ford! Hell, if I was your pet at least I'd be getting *fucked*!"

I raise my eyebrows at her.

She winces and backs away. "Sorry. Too far?"

I nod. "Let's go get my things from my apartment and I'll drop you off at home." I usher her out of the house and we get back in the Bronco and drive down to the shop.

It's not far, but I have a few boxes of stuff to load up, so I take the truck.

Ronnie sheepishly follows me upstairs to my apartment over the shop. It's pretty bare bones. Just some mismatched furniture and my leftover boxes of casual clothes and personal items. Ronnie grabs a box and I grab two, then we go back down to the Bronco and load it up.

She is silent the whole time. And I know why she's angry. Spencer is distant, but it's got nothing to do with her. He loves Veronica Vaughn. I know this, I've watched him with her on many occasions. And last summer when she accidentally got involved in that con we ran on Rook's ex, she almost got shot and Spencer was freaking out. That's how I know he loves her.

But I also know he'll never tell her as long as we have all this legal shit hanging over our heads. There's too many risks right now. We're all in this together—Rook, Ronin, Spencer, and me—until we know we won't be killed or put in jail.

And if certain people knew how much Spencer Shrike cares about Veronica Vaughn, then her life might be in danger too. And it's not fair to involve her. She's got nothing to do with any of these illegal jobs we've been doing.

We ride back to Fort Collins in silence and I'm still trying to figure out if I should call Spencer and tell him when I hang a right on Mountain Avenue. Ronnie is the only female member of the Vaughn family—which consists of her, her four brothers, her dad, and her grandfather. All of whom are tattoo artists and have owned a shop in Fort Collins called *Sick Boyz Inc.* since the early Sixties. They live in a gigantic old house in the historic district right off downtown. If I had left her at the restaurant she could've walked home in five minutes.

I almost feel bad for Ronnie. Spencer is serious about not involving her in the business and that means he does generally ignore her. And he's been especially aloof this past fall. But Ronnie has a point too. Why should she wait around for him if he's not providing for her?

I slow down to gather my thoughts because what I'm about to suggest might be a betrayal to one of my best friends and it takes a little getting used to. But Veronica's house comes into view and her brothers are all out in the front looking at one of their many cars, so I make a snap decision. "OK, look Ronnie. I won't tell Spencer because I get it. You're tired of waiting. I'll even hint around that you need some attention. And you're both going to Antoine's New Year's party, so you know for sure you'll see him then."

"I'm not even going as his *date*, Ford. Rook invited me, not Spencer! What if he brings a girl?"

"He's not gonna bring a girl to a party you'll be at, Ronnie. Don't be ridiculous." But in reality, Spencer is not all that astute when it comes to relationships. I might need to pull him aside and make sure he doesn't piss Veronica off. "Just give it until the trials are over in the spring, can you do that? Just wait a few months until all this legal shit is behind us?"

"I don't know, Ford. It just seems pointless."

"Well, at the very least, don't call him up and tell him. If you keep it secret, I'll cover for you. But shit, Veronica, if you push his buttons you know you'll piss him off and the first place he'll go is that guy's house. So I hope that banker has a gun."

She squints at me and then we're at her house. Her brothers descend on the Bronco like a pack of wolves and open her door.

"Ronnie where the hell have you been?" Vinn Vaughn, her middle brother, asks first.

"Ford," Vic, the oldest Vaughn brother says, "what the fuck are you doing with my baby sister?" All Ronnie's brothers are tatted up like, well, tattoo artists. Veronica has no tatts and that always surprised me. She's got a very strange blood phobia, so her continuing the trade never made sense. But she did get on board. She's one of them. And it was her talented hands who created Spencer's own body art. Every bit of it is Veronica's work.

"I saw her out jogging, picked her up and gave her a lift. She had a cramp in her side. She needs to work on her endurance." I look over at Ronnie when I say this. "Stamina, Veronica Vaughn. Slow and steady."

She smiles sweetly and looks me right back in the eye. "Thank you so much Ford, how about you stay for dinner?"

The Vaughn family is serious about their dinners and once you get invited, it's a done deal. You have no way out. Her brothers are on me like carrion. "Yeah, Ford. Come inside. The whole family's here. We got a little party going."

"Noooo—" But Grandpa Vaughn is already walking up to the Bronco waving at me.

Shit. How the hell do I start my day one hundred percent in control of this holiday and end up spending time with an old friend, buying presents from a cute kid, consoling my partner-in-crime's almost girlfriend, and invited over for dinner with the Vaughn clan?

I put the truck in park and give in.

Screw it. I still got five hours until my pet date and a man's gotta eat.

50

CHAPTER SIX

Christmas Eve dinner with the Vaughn family is not some sit-down with turkey and stuffing. No. It's a mass conglomeration of men and girlfriends milling about the house, drinking too much, smoking too much, and talking way too loud. Ronnie and I are the only ones with no dates. Even her grandpa has a lady friend over.

I think that's cute.

Ronnie's father, Vern, has the barbecue fired up and is cooking enough meat to feed a small village. I doubt there'll be leftovers.

I get jostled around between the various first floor rooms, talking to her brothers and then her grandpa—who fills my head with the most gruesome war stories I've ever heard—and then eat and make a swift exit. Swift is relative since I spend a few hours hanging out here.

Ronnie shoots me the stink eye as I wave goodbye to them.

Yeah, Spencer needs to take care of this shit. Because she is not happy. At all. And I don't blame her, he's being a selfish dick. He could at the very least explain himself.

I take College down to Harmony and hang a left towards the freeway. My apartment complex is down this way and I want to bring my computer home to fuck around with tonight after the pet leaves. I'm gonna look that guy up Veronica was with anyway. Just in case. If I never need to tell Spencer, fine. But it's better to have the info ready than be scrounging around for it after the fact.

There's almost no traffic today and I hit every green light all the way down to my apartment. I turn into the driveway and park in my spot. The jog up the steps feels good after so much driving today and I hope the snow isn't too bad tonight so I can run in the morning. Keep the routine. I like a routine.

The apartment is cold and empty. I never liked the place and if it wasn't for Spencer's guns hidden away in the third bedroom, I'd clear it out and be done with it. Chalk it up to a failed experiment with normalcy. But Spencer thinks it's necessary, so I paid up the rent for a year.

My phone buzzes in my jacket and I sift through the gifts and my new knife to find it. "Yes, Pam." She's my assistant in LA. Runs my whole life—from buying me clothes to setting up the pets.

"The studio called Mr. Aston. You're expected to show up on January fourth and pilot filming commences in New Zealand on the fourteenth for six weeks. Do you want me to book a flight for you on the third?"

"Well, that's good news, eh? We're finally getting somewhere with this shitty career." I sigh and take a seat on the couch as I picture leaving Denver for two months. I'm not ready to leave, to be honest. I'm not ready to let Rook go. I've enjoyed her too much and I've missed her even more this past month. I've barely seen her at all. Not since the last taping of Shrike Bikes. "Did we hear back from The Biker Channel on a Season Two?"

"Yes, sir. They said second week in March."

"During the trials?"

"Yes, sir. I think they specifically scheduled it that way for ratings."

"Of course they did. OK, well I'll call you back and let you know about the flight."

"Merry Christmas, Mr. Aston. If you need anything, I'm on call as usual."

"Yes, thank you, Pam." I press end and drop the phone on the cushion. Well, this is it. Life is changing. The only question is, what will I do with it?

I'm not sure yet. All I know is that I'm the only one of my inner circle that is spending this day alone.

Well, that's not quite true, I've seen a ton of people today. But all of them are home or on their way home. I'm the only one who has nowhere to go.

Well, that's not true either. My mother has a party every Christmas Eve and I'm always on the guest list.

But I'm not in the mood for a party and I'm not in the mood to go home. I'm avoiding home. But my reprieve is up. I have nowhere else to go. And maybe if I didn't have that pet coming over I might be tempted to sit Christmas out up here. There's no distractions. No one would look for me here. I'd definitely be left alone.

But after all these years of successfully spending Christmas by myself, I suddenly have some apprehension about it. And this apartment is not a good place to sit and get drunk. At least my Denver condo is in the middle of the city. I could go join other pathetic loners at whatever place is open. And there is always one place open nearby, no matter where I am in the world. There's always some bar owner who relates to us loners and agrees to house the rejected for a night of drowning away one's loneliness.

But the pet is coming over and if I'm being perfectly honest, I'm looking forward to her. She's not bad as far as pets go. She's got a nice body and she's trained well enough. So I grab my phone and my computer, and go back outside into the newly chilled air, climb into my Bronco, and head south.

The snow starts as soon as I hit I-70 and the drive into Denver is slick with ice as the wet roads freeze over. I get off the freeway and make my way down Broadway to my building. It's nine PM and I'm just getting into the turn lane when my phone buzzes.

"Now what the fuck?" I get stuck at the light so I grab my phone and find my mother's face staring back at me. I reluctantly press answer. "Hi Mom."

"Ford?"

"You called me, Mom. You know it's Ford. I'm the only son you have."

"It's just an expression, Ford. Can you go to the store and pick up some shallots? I thought I bought them yesterday, but they're not here."

"Shallots? Where the hell am I gonna find shallots at nine o'clock on Christmas Eve?"

"Eli's Market is open. I called him and he's waiting for you now, shallots in hand. He's that nice Jewish man—"

"I know who Eli is. He's lived next door to us for twenty years." I huff out a breath and then my turn light goes green. "Fine, I'll swing by Eli's and bring you some shallots."

I hang up, annoyed. It's a ploy, I know it. To get me to go to church. But it's not gonna work. I flip a bitch and make my way over to Park Hill where my mom's house is. Eli's Market is a couple blocks down from us, off Colfax.

Twenty minutes later I pull up to it and true to her word, Eli is standing there in the blowing snow, bag of shallots in hand. I pull up to him and roll my window down like this is a drive-up vegetable stand. "Thanks Mr. Maus," I say as I grab the bag, simultaneously hand him a twenty, and tell him to keep the change as I roll the window back up. I have forty minutes to get back home for my pet date.

Our street is lined with old trees that tower above the houses. Not all the houses are huge like ours. Spencer's, for example, is just a modest four bedroom bungalow.

Modest is not the word I'd use to describe our house. Pretentious, that's more like it. A huge American foursquare—which is almost a contradictory statement since foursquares are supposed to be humble. It has symmetrical windows on both the first, second, and third floors and I suspect this is why my mother wanted it. We both like orderly designs. The front porch is deep and massive, spanning the entire length of the house, with a wide, welcoming opening, and thick columns on either side. It's got seven bedrooms, six bathrooms, a carriage house where I lived for my senior year in high school, and an elaborate basement set up for dinner parties so the first floor can be used for chatting.

It's walled in with brick on all sides with a massive wrought iron gate that is at the moment open. There are parking attendants waving me off-property for parking, but I pull in anyway. I roll the window down and he immediately goes into his spiel about no parking in the driveway. "I live here. I'm pulling up, get out of my way."

Maybe my tone is a little much for a Christmas Eve party, or maybe he sees the flash of anger in my eyes—but his eyebrows go up in surprise and he moves off to the side. I pull up the driveway and park next to the kitchen door, then get out with my bag of shallots, and head inside.

It's like the North Pole threw up in here, that's how fucking festive it is. People are laughing, someone is playing Christmas songs on the piano in the front room, the whole house smells like food, and the commercial kitchen is packed with cooks and servers.

"Who needed shallots?" I call out to them.

They stare at me, and then ignore me.

"Right." I set the shallots down on the counter and go find my mother. Traditionally, foursquare homes are divided into four rooms per floor and includes the kitchen, the formal dining room, living room, and family room. Our living and family rooms have been remodeled so it's just one great room. My mother is standing in front of the windows, next to a man playing the piano. In fact, she's standing a little too close to this man playing the piano. She's laughing down at him with a twinkle in her eye and she's got a champagne flute in her hand.

Could my day get any more fucked up? Since when does my mother have a boyfriend?

Maybe if you came around more than twice a year you'd know.

People are talking to me as I make my way across the long front room but they know better than to touch me or get too personal, so I glide right past them and tap my mother on the shoulder.

My mother is kinda on the small side. Petite, I guess. She's got her auburn hair piled up on her head and she's wearing a conservative red dress that ends mid-calf. She turns and throws her hands up in excitement. "You made it!"

"No," I growl. "I came with your shallots but no one in the kitchen knows what I'm talking about."

"Oh," she turns to the man playing the songs. "Gary,

go tell the cooks what to do with the shallots, would you please?"

He gets up and leaves to do that I presume, and then my mother turns back to me with a smile. "I wanted you to meet him. Can you say hello at least?"

I just blink at her. "Meet him?"

"Yes, Ford," she says in her soothing mom voice. "I've been dating him for three months."

I turn away and walk out. I'm done with this fucking day.

I don't even know how I get back to my apartment garage, but I'm here already, sitting in my Bronco, trying to come to terms with what just happened. My mother has moved on.

Shit.

That fucking stings.

Like bad.

I check my watch and it's ten minutes past ten. Fuck. I grab my computer and get out. I jog over to the elevator, pressing the button repeatedly, hoping that will make it appear quicker. The doors finally open and I key in my penthouse code, then tap my foot the entire way up.

The doors open and the naked pet is walking to the closet on the far end of the hall where I have them leave their clothes. She stops mid-stride and stares at me, her brows a bit furrowed.

She might be pissed. I've left her waiting lots of times, but it *is* Christmas Eve.

"Sorry," I say as I quickly walk to my apartment door to unlock and open it. "If you're staying, follow me in, close the door behind you, and stand at attention."

I go inside and drop my keys on the foyer table and then walk straight to the office to lock up my computer.

The front door closes quietly behind me and her bare feet make a small padding sound as she walks into the living room.

I smile.

Finally. *Finally*, after all the bullshit I had to do today, I'm gonna get some satisfaction.

CHAPTER SEVEN

When I return to the living room my pet is standing ready in front of the window, not facing me. This is where I like them at night because the window is like a mirror and if they want, they can watch me walk up behind them. The rules state they will not look at me. But this pet cheats. Every single time. I can see her eyes trained on me like a target as soon as I appear in the living room. She knows I can see her and yet, she never bows her head—bowing is also against the rules and I'd definitely spank her for it tonight. I like an even chin with downcast eyes.

This is how I know she's playing a game. And not a sexual one, but a power one. Because if all she wanted was a spanking, she could bow her head and get it over with. But that's not all she wants. She wants me to punish her on her terms, but she's not in charge here. I am. So I've restrained myself for months.

I take my white t-shirt off as I walk up behind her. I can see the color of her eyes, green, that's how visible it is that she's watching me. Her lips part, form a seductive *o* shape, and the smallest of moans comes out as she licks her lips.

I squint my eyes down into slits as I consider what I'd like to do with her tonight. "Do you want to play, pet?"

Her eyes in the window lift up a little so she can stare into my own through the glass. "You know I can see you, so why do you do it?"

She looks away at this, but not because she was caught, but because she's thinking. Considering if she should risk talking.

If she talks, she's out. She knows this.

"Because you're trying to tell me something?" I guess.

She nods and holds my gaze.

"Because you're trying to tell me you're not a pet?"

She shakes out a no for this one and I let out a breath as I lean into her neck and nip the tender skin near her nape. "Right answer, pet. But is it true?"

She lets out a squeal and lifts her head. My hand automatically slides around the front of her throat. I palm it gently, then reach up under her jaw and press my thumb into the hollow under her ear, forcing her to turn her head towards me. She meets my gaze directly this time. In full defiance. And then she falters and takes a deep breath, letting it out slowly, to calm herself. "Do I make you anxious, pet?'

She swallows and nods.

"But you can leave any time you want. And yet you never do. Why?"

She squints her eyes at me.

"Why do you come here? Why do you let me treat you like this? Why do you put up with me?" I wait to see if she'll talk so I can throw her out and be done with it, but she holds her silence and redirects her gaze so it's not trained on me. I rest my hands on the top of her shoulders and she shivers as I push my chest into her back. My hands drop down to her nipples and I twist them, not hard, just enough to make her moan. One hand remains on her breast but the other caresses its way down her stomach and rests on her hip. "Come with me," I whisper in her ear.

I lead her over to the buffet table in the dining room and remove a pair of handcuffs from a drawer. She presents her hands behind her back before I even ask and my dick begins to grow as I fasten them carefully around her wrists. "You know what to do," I tell her softly.

She backs up a little, then bends over so her face is turned to the side, resting on the buffet, her arms are restrained is the small of her back, and her legs are slightly apart.

"Open your legs more, pet. I need to know you want it, or I'll send you home craving."

She widens her stance and then widens it again. Her eyes are open, looking up at me in defiance.

"Do you realize it's against the rules of play to look me in the eye?" I ask her.

She considers me, almost thoughtfully. Like I just asked her what she wanted for dessert. And then she nods yes.

"I should throw you out right now. Do you want me to be done with you?"

She shakes no.

"Then look away, *bitch*."

That word is like a slap and she closes her eyes, opens them, and redirects her gaze to the muted gray colored walls. I smack her hard on the left cheek as soon as she relaxes and she yelps. She's allowed to cry out in pain or pleasure, so I ignore this and pull her hair with my other hand, forcing her head back. "Now you may look at me, *whore*." She does. She knows my patience has run its course. "You want to press me? You want the nice

61

spankings? You want to come in here and try and control me?" My hand comes down hard on her ass and the redness appears at the same moment she cries out and pulls away. But I've still got a tight hold on her hair, so that snaps her back to attention.

I lean into her neck again and whisper, "You forgot to count, pet." And then I smack her twice and her fingers silently call out the numbers. *One. Two.* I pull her hair again and she whimpers this time. I've been rough with this pet before, but never angry. I rarely get angry, but I feel it tonight. I want to be angry.

I step back and take a breath because I don't want to send her away yet. I want to fuck this bitch. *Bad.* She's been testing me for months and she's still mine at the moment, so I will take her.

I need to get a hold of this anger, at least long enough to get off and send her on her way. I grab the key to her cuffs and turn towards the bedroom. "Follow." I call out as I walk away.

Her feet slap against the polished tiles as she runs to catch up with me. Once inside the bedroom I point to the bed. "Sit." She takes a resolving breath and sets herself atop the white down comforter.

Once again I ask myself why? Why the fuck do these bitches put up with me. I sit down next to her, close enough to make her whole body move with my weight on the mattress. "Lie across my lap." She puts her knees up on the bed and then bends over, sticking her ass way out because her hands are still bound behind her back, so she's forced to lower her face to my thigh and slide herself up into position. Which also forces her face to drag along my hardened dick, only the fabric of my jeans between her hot breath and my cock.

This takes the anger away a little because that right there, *that* was clever. And it tells me a lot of things. *One*—she's OK with my insults. *Two*—she's still not giving in to me, regardless of how well she's following the rules. And *three*—she wants to be fucked just as bad as I want to fuck her.

I'm not into being mean for the fuck of it. I like them to submit, that's all. I like to be in control. I like to call the shots. I like to be obeyed unconditionally. And almost all of the girls who make it beyond the first appointment do that, and do it well. But this girl has been skating on the edge of compliance the entire time she's been my pet. She needs to go. Tonight is her last night, so I'm going to enjoy her to the fullest before I send her packing.

I unlock her handcuffs and slide them off, tossing them on to the floor with a hard clunk.

"Ready, pet?"

She nods yes.

"I'm going to turn your cheeks bright red for your disobedience. But I'll make it worth it if you're a very good girl." She starts nodding her head when my hand comes down full force on her ass again, making both her legs kick up as she signs off a *one*. I slap them back down. "That's not a good example of perfect behavior, pet." I smack her again, harder, and this time she buffers the pain by sinking into my lap. I caress her ass for being good, rubbing her roundness, then stroking the back of her thighs, stopping in the dent behind her knee where I trace small, light circles.

She relaxes and I push her legs open, making one fall to the floor, and then smack her open pussy hard. My hand slips right between her legs and presses against her sex until she moans. I smack her again and now her entire ass is flaming red. Her hands do the sign for two. She lets off a sob and that means she deserves a gently probing finger around her asshole. She squeezes her hole closed, trying to take some control back, and I smack her hard enough to elicit a loud cry. "Don't. Your ass belongs to me and if I want to play with it, I will." I slip my finger inside and her whole body goes stiff, but she does not resist.

Victory for Ford.

I ease it out and grab her hair with the hand that has been holding her down. I force her head up by pulling and yes, sure enough, she's got tears. "You're defiant. I'm getting rid of you." She stares at me, then more tears come out and she looks like she might start wailing. I flip her over quickly and then move down the bed until her ass is flush with the edge of my thigh and her legs are draped over my lap. "You can get up and leave now if you want. You're never coming back. You refuse to submit and I'm tired of training you. It's a waste of time."

She's silent for a few seconds. "Or?" she asks quietly. Her voice is small and sweet. It's too bad, really. That she came here as a pet. I like her. But whatever her reason for being here, that in and of itself is enough to make me never want her in a serious way.

That and she's blonde.

They're always blonde or red because the last thing I want is any future woman I love to remind me of the shitload of pets I used up and threw away.

"Or I take away all the rules and we just fuck. All the dirty shit we've been doing is on the table. All of it. But when we're done, you leave and don't come back."

Her eyes narrow with her glare. "Why are you such an asshole?"

I laugh. "You can talk if you stay, but I'm not going to pretend I like you for your witty conversation. I like you for your pussy and I'd like to fuck you tonight. I'm tired of playing. Stay and have fun or get the hell out."

She stares up at me, then she bends her legs, points her toes, and lifts them up and back, wrapping her arms around her calves so her pussy is open to me.

I look down at her puffy lips, all swollen with desire and red with the rush of adrenaline in her system, and then I grab her ankles and push them towards her head so I can smack her clit. She cries out, her back arching up off the bed, and I smack her again, making her struggle to get free this time. I stand up and grab her arm before her legs can fall and then I turn her body around until her ass is hanging off the mattress, her feet on the floor.

I kick open her legs. She bites her lip and stifles a moan as I slide a finger into her sopping wet pussy and pump her hard before inserting another finger. "Oh God," she says, her voice heavy with desire.

"Did you get yourself off when you went home this morning?" She writhes as my fingers sweep back and forth against her sweet spot, then slide up and down her slit, rubbing her clit, creating the hard friction that has her panting out, "*Yes, yes, yes.*"

"Yes, you did?"

"*No*," she gasps as I thrust into her. "No, I didn't, but I want to come," she looks me in the eye. "Right now."

"No one's stopping you, pet." I lean down and tickle her nub with my tongue and suck until she screams and tries to clamp her knees closed. I push against her inner thighs and spread her wide open, sucking on her folds, her lips, her clit, and then tongue fuck her pussy until she gushes into my mouth and twists so hard she breaks free.

Her knees slide to the floor as her chest rests on the bed.

I take advantage of her presentation and stand her up so her ass is in the air and her lips are peeking through her closed thighs.

It's my turn to say, "*Yes*," now because this is how I like my women. I grab a condom from the nightstand, tear the wrapper open, and slide it down my cock. Then I stand up, lift her up by the knees and set them back down on the bed so her ass is at my waist. "Keep your head down and your ass up," I command. She's trying to answer me when I thrust into her, rocking her forward, her face sliding against the sheets. I smack her red ass and she yelps, squirming to get away. But I grab the front of her thighs and pull her towards me, burying myself inside her, all the way up to my balls. I fuck her like that, her crying out with each spanking, wriggling, only to have my arms clamp down on her—holding her still as she moans— begging me to make her come again.

My balls begin to tighten and just before I explode I reach around and stroke her clit, sending her into a screaming fit of "*Oh, oh ohhhhh.*" I push her forward on the bed and then collapse next to her and try to catch my breath.

My day suddenly sucks a little less.

I close my eyes and before I know it, I'm blinking awake as this fucking pet tries to rest her head on my chest.

I push her off me and sit up. "Time to go, girl. Out."

I don't wait for an answer, hell I don't even know if she's awake. I just get up and go to the bathroom, slipping the condom off and throwing it into the toilet before I start the shower. I glance down at the clock on my vanity. Fuck, it's only eleven. I waited all fucking day for forty-five minutes of sex.

It's hardly worth it.

"Mind if I join you," the ex-pet asks from the doorway. She's leaning against the door jamb, twirling her hair like she's trying to be sexy.

I narrow my eyes at her nerve. "I told you to go. There's no shower, there's no goodbye, there's no *Thanks for the fuck*. Just get out."

Her whole face changes with these words. It goes from soft and satisfied to chiseled hardness instantly. "I'm not sure who the hell you think you are or why you feel you're so special you can treat people like shit. But you know what? You're one disturbed, messed-up *freak*." She whirls around to leave but I catch her by the upper arm. My reaction surprises me but it positively scares the shit out of her. "Let me go," she growls. But I know her bravery is fake, I can feel her pulse quicken in her brachial artery.

My voice is calm when the words drip out. "*I'm* the freak? You're the one who shows up here, removes your clothes in my hallway, presents your pussy to me by lying on a mat in front of my door, and then allows yourself to be treated like shit just so you can what? Why the fuck would you ever agree to my conditions? Why? Other than you're a much more disturbed individual than I am. At least I'm the one who maintains some fucking dignity during our encounters. *You*—you just open your legs to a complete stranger. The same stranger you think is one disturbed messed-up freak. What you see in me is what you see in you. You're looking in the mirror, honey." I give her a shove towards the door and let go of her arm. "Now get out."

She lifts her chin up and smiles. I figure this is her pathetic attempt to save face, but there's a small gleam in her eye that says she really does feel superior. "Well, all that might be true. But if you really want to know why I do this, I'll tell you." She walks to the bedroom door to put some distance between us and then turns, still smiling as she drums her fingertips along the side of the door. "I do it because I need the money." And then she walks out.

What?

I pull my jeans back on and follow. She's already in the hallway half-dressed when I catch up with her. She buttons her jeans and slips her feet into her snow boots as she tugs the shirt over her head.

I stare at her. Hard. "I do not *pay* for sex."

"Right," she says pulling her hair out of her shirt and shrugging on her coat. "That may be true, but I certainly have been getting paid to show up here on command for the past two months." She huffs out a laugh. "What? You think you're so fucking special you can get nice girls like me to come be your sex slave just for the orgasms?"

I glare at her.

"I mean, sure, I had a few good ones. But come on? Get real, *Aston*. Pam pays me to come here, you dumbass. She pays all of us to service you and your fucked-up fetishes." She punches the button on the elevator and shoves her hands in her pockets. Then her gaze goes back to the pet mat. I follow that gaze because her expression becomes livid. "And you know what? I baked those fucking cookies for my kid. And you took one bite and threw that bag down on the ground like they were trash. Well, fuck you. I only do this job to pay for my babysitter while I go to school during the day, you self-absorbed, emotionless, pathetic excuse of a man. And my naive kid was the one who said I should bring my boss cookies on Christmas Eve to make him happy."

The elevator opens and she tugs her purse over her shoulder and enters. She doesn't look at me again, just hides in the corner where the buttons are and allows the doors to close without another word.

CHAPTER EIGHT

I seethe.

Positively seethe.

I want to call Pam up and fire her ass. I want to chase that little pet bitch down and fuck with her head, fill it with insults and half-truths so filled with venom, she'll need therapy for years to get over it.

I want to throw things through the fucking living room window.

I take a deep breath instead.

Because nobody. *Nobody*—especially not that skanky little cunt who sold her body for money—*nobody* can make me lose my temper.

It's just not possible. If there's one thing I control in my life, it's my reactions. I have complete control over my reactions and this bitch will not take that away. I take a deep breath and remember my shower is still running. I go back to the bathroom and strip, then douse myself in hot water to wash away the smell of slut.

When I'm done I wrap the towel around me and call Pam. She answers on the first ring. "I already heard. I'm so sorry, Ford."

That little tramp will not ruin my only real relationship I have in this world since my father died. Pam keeps my whole life from unraveling—she picks up all the slack. This woman holds me together professionally, and even if I'm not quite all there personally, no one ever knows because Pam is my cover. She's family to me and I would never throw away our five year working relationship over a *whore*. "Forget it, Pam. Forget it, OK? No more pets. Cancel all of them. I'm done." I end the call and the home screen flashes a missed call at me.

"Great." My fucking mother. I huff out a laugh. That's just what I need. To think about my mother and her new piano playing boyfriend. The asshole's probably a gold digger. *Prick*. I press the voice mail icon and it begins to play. *"Ford, I'm sorry. I don't want you to be upset. I've told Gary it won't work. I'm sorry."* She pauses here to sigh.

It's a *very* sad sigh.

"I have to get ready for church. Maybe you will find time to come by tomorrow? Have dinner?"

I press end. *Fuck*. This day has gone to shit. I pick up the remote and flip on the TV to break the suffocating silence. This TV came with the apartment. Biker Channel pays for this place, and this condo is one of the few luxury perks written into my contract. The local news comes on and I sit back to think.

Goddamn it. I run my fingers through my hair and glance at the clock. Not even midnight yet. The fucking day's not even over. I'm sure something else will go wrong if I just hang out a little longer. I might as well just go to bed. I point the remote at the TV to turn it off when I see the headlines. *Nine killed in military style- attack on home-grown terror cell west of Cheyenne.*

Holy shit, I totally deserve to see that. That's what I get for turning the TV on. I point at it again to turn it off and then stop.

The whole world fucking stops.

Sasha Alena Cherlin's face flashes across the screen. *Wounded in the firefight*, is all it says.

What fucking firefight?

I just stare at the TV for a few seconds, trying to process this new reality. Poor Sasha. I almost can't think straight as I try to come to terms with what this means for that smiling little girl this morning.

She sold me a present she bought for her mother, just so I could give it to my mother. And my mother will probably never see it because I'm an anti-social freak who can't bring himself to celebrate a holiday with his own family.

Family. That's something I take for granted, even after all that shit with my dad. I bet Sasha would kill to have a mother calling her up on Christmas Eve.

What kind of piece of shit am I?

I look back over at the clock. Eleven forty-two. I know where my mom will be in twenty minutes. Hell, she's probably there now. I walk back to my room and flip the light on in my closet. I put on a gray suit, comb my hair back, slip on my navy cashmere topcoat, and grab my keys and phone.

I'm going to church.

CHAPTER NINE

St. Margaret's is a traditional brick Catholic church with massive cathedral ceilings, dark wooden pews, the gigantic organ up in the corner, the lavish altar, and the stained glass windows. I haven't been in here in years, but as soon as I walk in the smell of incense overtakes my senses and I feel like I never left.

We have a spot where we sit. In fact, almost everyone has a *spot*. Midnight mass is tricky in this regard, because our spot on Saturday evening mass might be someone else's spot on Sunday morning. But when I look over at our spot, there's my mother.

Sitting alone.

I am such a bad son.

The interior is set up in a circular configuration. The altar is the top of the circle, then there are three sets of pews that span out from there. It's not a half-circle, even though that's the best way to describe it. It's slightly more than half a circle and to my mind, this never made sense. It bothered me when I was six and it bothers me now. I can't stand asymmetrical or uneven designs.

I do realize this is not normal. To hate this place because the architect wanted the pews to take up more than one-half of a circle so more people can fit in for the service. But I do. I *hate* this room.

It makes me uneasy just to be in here.

But I suck it up and walk to our pew and say, "Excuse me," in my most polite voice as I inch my way past the people already sitting in their *spots*, and plop down next to my mom. She likes to sit in the middle. Not just the middle of this section, or this pew, but the middle of the entire church.

I guess I take after her in that regard, because sitting here almost cancels out the uneven layout of the pews.

"Ford," she says in her soft church whisper voice. She leads by example and I was always a little too loud as a child, so that voice was practiced to no end.

"Sorry I walked out earlier. I didn't mean it the way it looked." I pause. "If it looked like I disapprove, then I didn't mean it that way. You have a right to be happy."

She looks up at me surprised.

"I hope he didn't stay away because of me. I'd feel terrible." Of course the reason she's alone is because of me, but it's done. Nothing I can do about that, so I don't dwell. She appreciates the sentiment and if the guy's worth a shit, he'll still be available tomorrow when she calls to smooth things over.

Then the choir starts up and the ceremony begins so our conversation is cut short. I look over at the section of pews at my left and through a small break in the crowd, I see Ronin smiling at me. Laughing at me, I think. Elise is on one side, and Antoine on the other side of her. And on Ronin's other side is Rook. She's belting out *Hark the Herald Angels Sing* like she owns it.

God, I love that girl.

She is my herald, a living proclamation that my life can get better.

Rook is so beautiful I constantly want to stare at her. Tonight she's wearing a cream colored suit and she has a red scarf around her neck. Her hair is down and flows over her shoulders in big bouncy curls. She looks up for a moment, to watch the priest and his attendants ascend the steps to the altar, and her bright blue eyes flash in the low light.

She takes my breath away. I reluctantly redirect my gaze over to the other side of the church where Spencer's family sits. Mass begins as I gawk at all the familiar faces. Spencer's parents are still together and they sit on either side of him. He's an only child as well, which was why we gravitated to each other as children. His eyes wander my way and when he spots me sitting in the pews, he fakes an exaggerated look of surprise. Or maybe not so exaggerated, since I haven't been here in years. Then he shoots me with his finger and someone behind me flicks my ear.

Spencer laughs when I wince but I don't even turn around. I know who it is. Sister Anne Catherine.

My childhood nemesis.

She does not accept my silent surrender and leans in to whisper, "Rutherford, behave yourself."

My mother looks over at me with disapproval, Spencer shoots his finger again and covers his fake laughing mouth like he's ten, and when I look over at Ronin he's smirking.

Rook is reading the bulletin intently, like she's studying for a test.

God, I love her.

My heart begins to beat wildly and I suddenly have the need to flee, but my mother grabs my coat sleeve when I make to rise and I settle back down.

"You're here now, Ford," she whispers. "Just relax and enjoy it."

And that is how I spend the wee hours of Christmas Day. Desperately wishing I was anywhere but church as I kneel, sit, stand, wish Sister Nemesis peace, and then force myself not to freak out when she grabs my hand to shake it.

She does that on purpose.

There's no way I'm taking communion, so as soon as our row gets up for it, I pat my mother on the shoulder as my only warning, and make my escape out the back. I stuff my hands into my coat pockets, sorta proud of myself that I lasted a whole hour in there, and then spy Ronin's black truck across the street from my Bronco.

I could put Rook's present in the truck. I walk over to the Bronco and open up the glove box.

Oh, God. Looking at Sasha's gift wrapping handiwork almost makes me feel sick. What must she be thinking right now. I grab both presents and my knife and stuff them all in my pockets. I jog back over to Ronin's truck. The doors are locked but the back glass window slides open when I try it. I hop in the bed, reach my hand in, and drop the little Eric Cartman package on her seat.

I hope she doesn't sit on it, but if she does, she'll definitely know it's there. I close the window and hop out, then spy my mom's Mercedes down the street. Sasha would definitely be disappointed in me if I never gave that bracelet to her. And since I'm not sure if I'll go home tomorrow for dinner—that's asking a lot, even if it is Christmas—I better drop it off now, too.

I have a remote on my key chain that unlocks her car, so I slip in the driver's seat and prop the little gift bag in the ledge of her GPS console and then get out and lock it up.

I feel a little bit like Santa Claus and some of the dread and unease melts away as I walk back to my Bronco. I pocket my gift-wrapped knife and drive home. It stopped snowing and the sky is clear and black, with more stars showing than you usually see in the city.

When the elevator opens to my penthouse hallway, I'm half expecting that psycho-pet to be here waiting, but she's not. I'm alone again. I'm not sure how getting rid of the pets will affect me. I'm not even sure if I'm serious about it. I'll probably call Pam up tomorrow begging for one. Surely she can't have scheduled one for Christmas Day. There's still time if I want to change my mind.

I'm just not sure.

I hang up my coat and change out of my suit and into some sweats and a t-shirt.

What a fucking day.

I pour some whiskey into a rocks tumbler and take a long slow sip. This is what I've needed since this morning. Teach me to drive all over two fucking states. My phone buzzes an incoming call and I look at the time. Almost one thirty. And it's my mom.

"Mom?" I ask, like she does every time I call as if she didn't have caller ID and know for a fact that it's me.

"Ford," she says with a lightness in her voice. "You have caller ID, why do you always ask if it's me?"

I laugh.

"I just wanted to thank you for the gift, Ford. It's lovely. And who may I ask is Sasha?"

My laugh dies. I forgot she signed the card. "She's a kid who sold me the necklace." I tell my mom the story of where it came from because Sasha would've wanted me to, and I can tell she's choked up about it. I even tell her what happened with her dad and the news broadcast. My mom is smart. She's not delusional, she knows what I do. She knows that somehow I'm connected to this girl's father. She knows Spencer, Ronin, and I are guilty as fuck of just about everything they say about us on TV. She knows. But she accepts me. My parents have always accepted me. The weirdness was never a factor. We chat for almost eight minutes. I don't think I've ever talked to my mother on the phone for so long in my life.

"I'm so sorry that happened, Ford," she says as the conversation winds down.

"Yeah, me too. I might drive up there tomorrow and see if she needs anything so you should probably just get Gary to come keep you company all day."

She sighs. "I miss your father every day, Ford. I do. He was my whole life. But he's been gone for two years now and I'm lonely."

I nod, like she can see me. "I understand. It's OK." I'm not really sure that it is OK, but she needs to hear that, so I say it anyway. I'm not capable of much empathy, but I can fake it. And they never know the difference, so what the fuck. It doesn't cost me anything to pretend to understand and be nice.

We say our goodbyes and hang up.

CHAPTER TEN

Everything seems to be changing all of a sudden. This morning I had a routine. I'm not sure if it was a good routine or a healthy one, but it was there. Running, pets, Pam.

And now, I'm not sure where I am, let alone where I'm going.

I turn the TV off and leave my whiskey on the coffee table. My bedroom feels sterile to me. The only hint that someone actually sleeps here is the rumpled duvet from my earlier fuck with psycho-pet. I'm just about to turn off the light and give up on this day when my phone buzzes.

What could my mother want now?

I pick it up and look at the face.

Rook.

My whole life gets better in an instant.

"Miss Corvus." The words rumble out in my smooth Ford voice I save just for her. "I realize you don't need beauty rest, but some of us do."

She snorts at me. "Ford, you are so, so stupid! I just called to tell you I found this little Eric Cartman toy on my seat. In fact, I sat on it and it made me jump." I picture this in my head and I wish I was there to see it. "And imagine my surprise when I opened it and found that card."

Busted. I didn't write the card. Sasha did. "I have no idea what you're talking about. Tell me what the card says."

"It says," she stops to clear her throat. "*To Ford's friend who is a girl. He likes you a lot, but I'm gonna try and steal his heart when I get my braces off, so you better move fast. Merry Christmas, Sasha and Ford Forever. XXOO, heart, heart, flower.*"

I laugh. I laugh so hard it echoes off the walls in this stupid ultra-modern condo. "Well," I tell her, "that pretty much made my whole day. If I could have you and Sasha together, my life might be complete."

"I got you something too, Ford. But I was afraid to call it a gift. Ronin says you don't like holidays."

"Some people make some holidays more tolerable than others. What did you get me?"

She takes a deep breath. "I talked Ronin into letting me do another season of Shrike Bikes. But I'm not gonna do it unless you're the producer. So if you're out, I'm out too. Because I never realized how much we do together until we were separated this month. When I don't run with you every day, I feel a little lost. You kinda ground me, Ford. I need it. I need that show and I'm really looking forward to all of us being together again."

I breathe deeply to calm my racing heart. "I just heard today that Season Two is on. My assistant called from LA and said they want to film during the trials. I know it'll be hard, but we'll manage it, OK? Ronin, Spence, and I will make sure we come out of this looking squeaky clean."

"I've never doubted you guys, Ford. Never. I look at my life today and I think to myself—Rook, how the hell? Ya know? Just how the hell did you get here? Remember when you asked me that last summer?"

"Yeah," I say as I think back to that day. I was falling in love with her and I didn't even know it. "Last Christmas I was in Japan, all alone, producing a game show. Two Christmases ago I was still enjoying the fact that I had two parents, even if I did take them for granted. Three Christmases ago I was fighting with Ronin and Spencer so bad, we stopped talking completely. Four Christmases ago Mardee was dead from an overdose. Five Christmases ago I was running cons with Ronin and Spencer like we were invincible. I feel like I'm going in circles, ya know? Ending up right back where I started. But you, Rook. You've changed my life."

I stop there because I'm very close to telling her how I really feel and I'm not gonna confuse her like that on Christmas. She loves Ronin, not me. If I was a good guy I'd leave her the fuck alone, just move on to my next job and get over it.

"Well," she says to slice through my silence. "Five Christmases ago I thought Wade Minix was my forever guy. Four Christmases ago I thought Jon Walsh was my forever guy. Three Christmases ago I was getting the shit beat out of me by my soon-to-be husband. Two Christmases ago I thought I was going to be a mom." She stops here to pull herself together and it almost breaks my heart listening to her talk about the baby she lost. "And last Christmas we had this big party at our house in Illinois. It was a nice party actually, but I can only really remember two things. My body was very sore from Jon beating me the night before and I was very cold because I was standing outside in the middle of the night, looking up at the stars. Like I am right now."

"You're outside?"

"Mmmhmm. I saw this star that night. It was so, so

83

bright. And it had a bluish color to it. And maybe I've never really looked before, but I've never seen a blue star. It struck me as special, ya know?"

I grab my coat from the front closet and slip outside on my balcony so I can look at the stars as she talks. "I'm outside now too. It's fucking cold out here, Rook!"

"I know. But I wanted to look for that star when I called you, can you help me find it?"

"Was it in the south?"

"Ummm, yes, I think. I was standing next to Jon's car, looking up over the trees behind the house. That's South, right?"

I don't want to think about that house but I force myself to picture it on the satellite image Spencer and I used to find Rook when she took off last fall. "Yeah, the woods were south, so you would've been looking southwest. Where are you now? On Ronin's balcony or the garden terrace?"

"Garden terrace."

"Walk over and look at Coors Field."

"OK"

"Then look left a little bit, then up at the sky. It's twinkling tonight."

"I see it! Oh my God, Ford, how do you know this shit?"

How I love to make this girl happy. I've never wanted someone to be happy so much in my life. "It's called Siriuo. It's the brightest star in the sky and it's prominent in the winter. An educated guess, that's all."

She's silent for a few seconds. "I wished on that star, Ford. I asked Santa Claus or God or someone, it didn't matter to me who it was. I just wished on that star and I asked it to make my life change. Because I couldn't live like that anymore, Ford. I was thinking bad things last Christmas. It was a very dark time for me. But I wished on that star that my life would change. It didn't even have to be a *good* change, but it just couldn't stay the same. And it did. I took a lot of chances. I accepted a lot of risk to get here, but here I am. I feel like I'm home now."

I nod, but inside I'm devastated. "I understand, Rook, I do."

Ronin's voice calls out to her from a distance. He must be in the doorway to the studio.

"Well, that ball and chain is barking at me to come inside and go to bed. Will I see you tomorrow, Ford?

There is nothing I want more than to see you tomorrow. I want you every day. These words try to come out, but I hold them back with great difficulty. "No, I think I have plans tomorrow. With a girl up in Wyoming."

"Would that be Sasha?" she chuckles.

"Yeah—" I want to tell Rook everything. Every single thing that happened to me today from Merc to Sasha, to Veronica and Spencer, and my mom and her new boyfriend. So much happened today and I have no one to share it with. No one. I just want someone to listen to me for once.

"You'll be at the New Year's Party for sure, though, right? Exit interviews for Shrike Bikes Season One? You know how I hate those…"

"Yeah," I say softly. "I know. And for sure I'll be there."

"OK, Ford. Merry Christmas. I'll see you soon. Bye."

The phone beeps that the call has ended and I'm alone again. I look up at Rook's Christmas star and make my own wish. I need something new. I need *someone* new. I need change, good or bad, like Rook said. I just need *this life* to stop being mine.

I take a deep breath and go back inside to my totally empty, ultra-modern, sterile, cold and lonely condo.

The knife I bought from Sasha is still wrapped up in pretty Christmas bows and paper, so I pick it up and sit on the couch to open it. I untie the gold ribbon and then carefully peel back the red paper. It's stupid to be excited, I know what the gift is, I bought it for myself. But even so, Sasha made it special.

Inside the case is the Mini CQC. But that's not all that's in there. I smile as I pick up the silver flash drive all decorated up with mini stickers. Snowflakes, Santa faces, reindeer, and a few guns.

Fucking Nikita.

I grab my computer from the office and set it on the coffee table so I can plug the drive in and see what's on it. It can't be anything personal, she didn't have time. But the curiosity is killing me.

It's got an autorun program that pulls up a welcome screen. It's bobbleheads with transposed pictures of Sasha and her father's faces on them, bobbing their heads to Jingle Bells.

The menu almost breaks my heart. This must be a photo CD of trips Sasha and her dad took. I click a link and it cycles through a series of images set to Christmas music.

I bet that little girl is kicking herself for giving me this drive. I get my external drive with my scripts on it out of the bedroom safe and run a Wyoming DMV crawl for the name Cherlin. There's a few of them, one in Cheyenne, obviously Sasha's father. A few in Laramie, obviously not cattle ranches since they are within city limits on the satellite map. And one family up in Big Horn, just south of Sheridan. I memorize the address and blow out a long breath of air

Sasha will never have another happy Christmas. She will never live through this day without thinking of how her father was killed, how she was left in a cabin to wait it out, how she ended up in the hospital—*orphaned.*

I can't do this anymore. I can't do this. I can't be this guy, I can't live this life, I can't stay here tonight. I walk into my bedroom and stuff a backpack full of clothes. I grab my toothbrush and some toiletries, shoving them inside as well. And then I pull on a pair of jeans and a hoodie, shrug myself into my boots and leather jacket, and walk out the door.

I can't change the fact that Sasha got her dad taken away from her on Christmas Eve, but I can be the guy who shows up on Christmas Day, trying his best to make this fucked up shit just a little bit easier.

End Of Book Shit

Welcome to the End of Book Shit for Slack. Back when I first published Slack in December 2013 the EOBS wasn't what it is today. So it was short and kinda stupid. Lol. So it's appropriate, and fitting that I take a moment and write down a few thoughts about what came next in this fictional world and how Slack was actually the beginning of Everything, with a capital E.

Slack started out as a character study of Ford. See... people kinda fell in love with this guy as they got to know him better in the Rook & Ronin trilogy. I had no clue Ford would end up being one of my most loved characters of all time. He still has a very special place in my heart, even though dozens of great characters and stories have come after him. There is just something very appealing about a guy who can't be broken... breaking.

He didn't break much in this story. It was more of a crack, really. Yes, he was hurting over Rook. And who hasn't been there, right? Everyone has lost in love before. Even if you've been married to your high-school sweetheart for fifty years, there was probably someone in the background who rejected you. Maybe it was just a passing crush on the "popular guy" in school, or something as seemingly stupid and insignificant as the boy who sat next to you in kindergarten. Either way, we all know that feeling.

I think that's why people related to Ford the way they did. I think his confession at the end of panic made readers sit up straight and say, "Who, hold on a second. What the fuck is happening?"

But in Slack he's not very sympathetic. I mean... Pets? Come on, Rutherford. What the fuck is that?

And then we get to Merc. This is Merc's very first appearance in the epic thirteen-book story that these books would eventually become. He's kina odd. Kinda funny. Kinda dangerous. But you only get a glimpse of him, because the star of those scenes isn't Merc, it's Sasha.

To be clear, I had no idea that The Company was going to be my net series. None at all. I just knew Ford wasn't on the up and up, had a dangerous friend called Merc, and stumbled into this little girl totally by accident.

But Sasha made it very clear she wasn't gonna be left behind. She was immediately intriguing to me. Immediately calling for more story. So when I decided to kill her father at the end and send Ford up to Wyoming to try and make things right, I did it with something in mind.

And what a something she became.

She is the star of The Company, Sure, James Fenici is why bitches pick up, but when they put it down, it's Sasha's story they need.

She's just... that kind of character. A lot like Ford, actually. Someone who has more to say then the pages they've been confined to.

If you want more Sasha, keep reading. The book, order, after this one are:

Taut

Bomb

Guns
The Company
Meet Me In The Dark
Wasted Lust
Happily Ever After
And if you want to take a little side journey into another world running parallel to Sasha's, pick up 321 as well.

The journey continues kids, so keep reading. Taut is up next.

Book five in this series is called Taut. And it's the real Ford Aston story. And books six and seven are called Bomb and Guns and they're about Spencer and Veronica.

Guns is the complete ending of the story arc of Rook, Ronin, Ford, Spencer, and Veronica. And a few new characters too—Ashleigh, Sasha, James, and Merc. All of whom intersect in the book called The Company and standalones called Meet Me In The Dark and Wasted Lust.

So if you're looking to enter a WORLD. If you're looking to meet characters so real, you feel like you know them. If you're looking to go on the ride of your life with Rook and her friends, keep reading, bitches.

I got you.

Book two in this series is called Manic and it's the beginning of Rook's unraveling... book three is called Panic, and it's the beginning of how she ravels it all back up.

Books four and five are called Slack and Taut, respectively. They're about Ford Aston, who you haven't met yet, but if you read book two, you will pretty quick. And books six and seven are called Bomb and Guns and they're about Spencer and Veronica.

Guns is the complete ending of the story arc of Rook, Ronin, Ford, Spencer, and Veronica. And a few new characters too—Ashleigh, Sasha, James, and Merc. All of whom intersect in the book called The Company and standalones called Meet Me In The Dark and Wasted Lust.

So if you're looking to enter a WORLD. If you're looking to meet characters so real, you feel like you know them. If you're looking to go on the ride of your life with Rook and her friends, keep reading, bitches.

I got you.

Thank you for reading, thank you for reviewing, and I'll see you again in the new EOBS of Taut.

Julie
JA Huss

About The Author

JA Huss never wanted to be a writer and she still dreams of that elusive career as an astronaut. She originally went to school to become an equine veterinarian but soon figured out they keep horrible hours and decided to go to grad school instead. That Ph.D wasn't all it was cracked up to be (and she really sucked at the whole scientist thing), so she dropped out and got a M.S. in forensic toxicology just to get the whole thing over with as soon as possible.

After graduation she got a job with the state of Colorado as their one and only hog farm inspector and spent her days wandering the Eastern Plains shooting the shit with farmers.

After a few years of that, she got bored. And since she was a homeschool mom and actually does love science, she decided to write science textbooks and make online classes for other homeschool moms.

She wrote more than two hundred of those workbooks and was the number one publisher at the online homeschool store many times, but eventually she covered every science topic she could think of and ran out of shit to say.

So in 2012 she decided to write fiction instead. That

year she released her first three books and started a career that would make her a New York Times bestseller and land her on the USA Today Bestseller's List eighteen times in the next three years.

Her books have sold millions of copies all over the world, the audio version of her semi-autobiographical book, Eighteen, was nominated for an Audie award in 2016, her book Mr. Perfect was nominated for a Voice Arts Award in 2017 and her book Taking Turns was nominated for an Audie award in 2018.

She also writes book and screenplays with her friend, actor and writer, Johnathan McClain. Their first book, Sin With Me, will release on March 6, 2018. And they are currently working with MGM as producing partners to turn their adaption of her series, The Company, into a TV series.

She lives on a ranch in Central Colorado with her family, two donkeys, four dogs, three birds, and two cats.

If you'd like to learn more about JA Huss or get a look at her schedule of upcoming appearances, visit her website at www.JAHuss.com or www.HussMcClain.com to keep updated on her projects with Johnathan. You can also join her fan group, Shrike Bikes, on Facebook, www.facebook.com/groups/shrikebikes and follow her Twitter handle, @jahuss.